For Stella & Paul,

with love,

Francine

WOMEN
and

CHILDREN

Bigfoot Dreams

Hungry Hearts

Household Saints

Animal Magnetism

Marie Laveau

The Glorious Ones

Judah the Pious

W O M E N

and

C H I L D R E N

STORIES

Francine Prose

PANTHEON BOOKS

NEW YORK

Some of these stories first appeared, in somewhat different
form, in The New Yorker, Antaeus, Atlantic, Pushcart
Prize XI, Commentary, and Ploughshares.

Library of Congress Cataloging-in-Publication Data
Prose, Francine, 1947–
Women and children first, and other stories.
I. Title.
PS3566.R68W66   1988   813'.54   87–25827
ISBN 0–394–52767–4

Book design by Chris Welch
Manufactured in the United States of America
First Edition

For Sara Bershtel

CONTENTS

T I B E T A N

T I M E

Most of the Buddhists were therapists from the Upper West Side. Milling awkwardly in the small lobby outside the temple, the ones who seemed to know each other were being especially friendly to the ones whose nametags they had to check. The women were rather quiet and smiled pleasantly while the men discussed how long some Tibetan lamas live. A young man with a ponytail said,

"There's lots of monks in Lhasa who claim to be over a hundred. Hey, it's Lost Horizon *city* up there."

A gray-haired man in a blue parka, one of the few not wearing a nametag, said, "Well . . . in *Tibetan* time. Who knows how those guys keep track. They're not exactly punching in the forty-hour week."

"Or the fifty-minute hour," another man said, and quite a few people chuckled.

Ceci was acutely aware of how strongly she smelled of perfume. Yesterday, on her way home from work, she had stopped at a bookstore on Eighth Street, leafed through a fashion magazine till she was the only one at the rack, then surreptitiously unfolded a perfume ad, rubbed the scented strip on both wrists, and put the magazine back. She'd thought: How peculiar. She was spending the evening alone. But wasn't that same magazine always telling you to do little things just for you? It was a designer scent, florid, with a musky edge of the dry cleaner's. She'd washed her hands at home this morning, and again in the bathroom after the two-hour bus trip here. Why hadn't it come off? She was sure others smelled it, too, and were dismissing her because of it as a completely unserious Buddhist.

One by one, the newcomers were being drawn out on the subject of what they did for a living and why they'd come down, mostly from Manhattan, for the all-day meditation retreat. When Ceci said she taught kindergarten at a private school in the Village, the slackening of attention was palpable. That was how she knew that few of the Buddhists had kids. Luckily she was the last to be asked; as to her reasons for being here, she could say what the others said. They'd said interest, curiosity. A few said that certain questions kept coming up in their practices. One man said, "So many of my clients seem terrified of some emptiness, and I know that for Buddhists emptiness is what you're shooting for. Plus, I've heard the Lama is pretty therapeutically sound."

An elderly German woman said she used to travel a lot; now she was homesick for the incense and bells. "It has been years since I heard a good old Katmandu bonnng," she said, and made a temple bell gong in her mouth.

Not one person said: I needed to get out of the apartment, I needed a day in the country with other people. Yet many looked pale and chapped, with red noses and brittle, brownish-gray hair; they looked like they'd been indoors too long. For all Ceci knew, every one of them might be like her, crying at night, weeping into the pillow like a sixteen-year-old. She wondered how many of them had picked this retreat as she had, from a newspaper ad. Under the Dharma Center ad was an ad for a travel bureau. If Ceci had had the time and the money she would have taken the charter flight to Negril.

And yet she was glad that she'd come, and that she had paid the extra fifty dollars for a private interview with Lama Sakuro, the Tibetan master visiting the U.S. When she sent in her money, she had imagined telling the Lama that her husband had left her and taken a job at an observatory in Arizona. She would ask: How could she be so surprised that he meant what he'd said all along? He really was an astronomer first. He really didn't want kids. She would ask what you did when you realized that your life will never turn out like you planned. Obviously she was going to the Lama the way other people visited storefront fortunetellers, only the Lama was safer—unlikely to offer to remove the curse from her money, or anything like that. What did she know about Buddhism? Prayer wheels, rock gardens, the Dalai Lama—she knew what everyone knew.

These Buddhists seemed very keyed up about their upcoming interviews with the Lama. The oldtimers swaggered a bit. They'd seen the Lama many times, always when they had reached some stage in their spiritual progress and wanted permission to take on a new practice. Each managed to mention how long it had been since they'd taken refuge in the dharma. They all agreed that the Lama kind of pooh-poohed the theoretical. He was better at giving out meditations. One woman said that this had been the hardest thing to understand—that the words themselves had power. But what the Lama told her was, they'd worked for three thousand years. Several people nodded at this. The man in the parka said, "The people who get into trouble are the ones who think the Lama's going to be some kind of fortune cookie."

Ceci wondered: How does he know about me? But of course there must be lots like her. And what was so bad about that? It occurred to her that for many people, the moment before they crack into a fortune cookie is probably the closest they ever come to a moment of genuine spiritual awe, of facing destiny straight on. Once, in a Chinese restaurant, she'd reached for a fortune cookie and her husband had grabbed her hand and asked if, sight unseen, she would trade fortunes with him. It made her a little anxious not knowing exactly whose fortune was whose, but finally she was just flattered that he wanted anything of hers. Last month she read in a magazine about a Chinatown luncheonette where one of the cooks was a pharmacist—sea horses, reindeer tusks, that sort of thing.

Now the place had a new crowd of regulars: the dying, alone or with friends.

From the temple came the velvety sound of a gong, less a sound than a feeling, like an enormous Q-tip stroking the length of your spine. No one spoke till the sound died out, a fading-away that lasted so long that by the end, everyone had sheepish smiles, which brightened considerably when someone said, "Lunch!"

There were two factions: the Buddhists who only talked about Buddhism and the ones who made small talk. The more worldly ones seemed embarrassed, as if the serious ones were their slightly out-of-it siblings who might alarm the new visitors. Every time one of the first type said something like, "Well, basically, it's all illusion," the others would let that remark pass and then compliment the food, an excellent curried ratatouille with crusty baguettes and butter. The German woman said, "This is some dining room"—which it was: handsome, wainscotted, grand enough for twenty people to fit around a long oak table, but also attractively rough; dust motes streamed in the gold, vintage-photograph light. The worldly Buddhists took turns explaining how the rambling building was originally a boardinghouse for workers who'd come to dig the reservoir nearby. A soft-spoken woman named Beth said, "And the Indians. This place was apparently a healing spot for the Indians."

"You know what the Lama eats?" the ponytailed kid said. "Barley gruel. Even when there's food like this already made, he has his cook stew him up a plain bowl of barley gruel."

"It's what works for him," said the man in the blue parka. "What makes him run. You don't put diesel fuel in a Cadillac." Everyone passed around condiment jars. It struck Ceci as a good sign that the Buddhists ate with such gusto. She did what they did, smeared Thai basil and chili paste with butter on the French bread. Down the table, they were discussing the Tibetan diet: leaden dumpling soup, sausages stuffed with sheep fat and red pepper. Though Ceci ate greedily, she felt she was growing smaller, becoming that invisible person whom no one expected to interact with the group. Out in the world, every one of these people was someone's slightly out-of-it brother or sister; but here they had found each other, and Ceci was on her own. The first to finish lunch, she stood up and excused herself with the lamest of lame, self-erasing smiles.

She drifted into the small lobby and perched on the edge of an antique rattan couch. On the coffee table were three books. She picked up the smallest one first. *Lotus Perfection*, by Lama Suravindo, in paperback with thin pages and blurry print, from the Samskara Press, New Delhi. She soon exchanged this for a large glossy picture book of Tibet and turned past the photogenic yurts, the prayer flags with the blue sky and white Himalayas behind them, past the masked demon dancers in the temple courtyard, straight to the wedding party. At first glance the bride looked so pretty, pink-cheeked, in her embroidery, striped blankets, tons of silver and turquoise and coral jewelry. Then you saw that she was terrified, and about twelve.

The third book was an offset-printed local history of the reservoir. In one of its few photos, reservoir workers, dressed up in shirtsleeves and derbies, posed on a lawn. It gave Ceci a funny chill when she recognized the monastery behind them. The men were young, and all seemed eager to appear jaunty, but many looked wild in the face, frightened, their eyes as black and buttonlike as the Tibetan bride's.

As the Buddhists came in from lunch, the German woman who was homesick for temple bells was talking about her travels. The man in the parka trotted beside her, asking questions, while soft-spoken Beth— who was, Ceci gathered, the parka man's wife—trailed miserably behind. The man told the German woman, "You know, you remind me of Alexandra David-Neel." A long look passed between them, and the German woman said, "What a compliment. Joe Namath may be your hero, but Alexandra is mine. *Magic and Mystery in Tibet* is my bible."

Joe Namath? The parka man hardly seemed the type, but still he nodded agreeably. His wife sulked. Naturally Ceci was on her side. How could Beth meditate and still keep an eye on that? Ceci thought of her husband's last letter. He described stopping at a Denny's on the way to Phoenix and seeing a young woman by the door, pacing, looking for someone, a little frantic. The woman was beautiful and glanced at him, but they didn't speak. When Ceci's husband left the restaurant—he wrote this in the letter—he felt a devastating sense of loss, that he had lost his entire life by passing that woman by. Two hundred miles down the road he still longed to turn and drive back. How was Ceci supposed to answer that?

She'd wanted to write back: Listen. That woman was me. For wasn't that how they'd met, in the lobby at the Museum of Natural History, where she'd gone with her class and was chasing after a stray child? Her husband, who was there to consult with someone on the staff, had looked at her and kept looking. Maybe that was a technique he'd learned for searching out new galaxies: you just focused on a spot and waited. But she didn't write that, didn't write anything, because it was so obvious: the woman in Denny's wasn't her. It was someone else entirely.

Another gong sent everyone straight to the den; probably they had their own name for this pine-paneled room, with its brown linoleum floor and colonial maple couches. They sat on the sofas and, when the chairs were full, on the floor. Ceci was the only one wearing shoes. What had the others done with theirs, and when? The man in the parka said, "I'd like to start by welcoming those of you who are new to the Dharma Center. My name is Walter. We will begin with ten minutes of meditation." He took off his Swatch and set it on the floor in front of him, a gesture Ceci found comforting. The Buddhists took this opportunity to straighten their backs and cross their legs—the serious ones in full lotus—and upturn their hands on their knees. Ceci took off the black leather sneakers she'd bought on Fourteenth Street and tucked them uncomfortably under one thigh.

Ceci closed her eyes and opened them. No one else's eyes were open, except for the kid in the ponytail, but at least his gazed blindly ahead, not scanning the room like hers. She shut her eyes again and thought: All right. Ten minutes to think. But what were the others thinking? She couldn't ignore the breathing, its measured intake and fall. After a while she heard someone's stomach growl.

Finally Walter looked at his watch and smiled and hit a kind of mini-gong. There was a lot of shoulder shifting and neck rotating. Walter handed out a mimeoed sheet. "I think this explains itself," he said. "We'll use the next hour to talk about the dharma. Then a short break, then a half-hour sitting meditation, then individual sessions with the Lama, then final meditation. Then dinner—and a party!"

Walter let the smiles die out. Then he said, "I thought we might begin by talking about suffering and desire." He spoke with the faintest trace of an accent, every slow, soft word a testament to how unhurried and at peace he was. Whenever he quoted the Buddha, his voice got even lower. "What it all boils down to is, suffering comes from desire."

Ceci thought of Walter's wife, sulking while he chatted up the German woman; her only desire was for her husband not to flirt with a woman who, though elderly, still had terrific cheekbones. But didn't that prove it? Suffering came from desire. Even the memory of desire was enough. When Ceci remembered her husband, there were certain places, certain nights and times she was careful to avoid. But finally you couldn't predict when your own desires would jump up out of nowhere and hurt you. On the bus down from New York, Ceci had sat across the aisle from a mother and her beautiful four-year-old son. "Kitty cat," the mother called him. "Sugar pops." She kept stroking his hair, patting his head, scrubbing her knuckles along the back of his blue satin baseball jacket. Ceci had had to watch that.

Walter said, "The way to stop suffering is to give up our attachments. Attachments to things we want. To what we already have and are afraid of losing. And what's left is: living right. Dying right. Following the dharma without attachment or desire."

The kid in the ponytail said, "I hear where sometimes the Ethiopians don't want the rice any more. They tell the planes not to come. They know they're dying; dying's their business and they want to get on with it." There was an uneasy silence. No one looked at anyone else.

"Everyone suffers," said Walter. "As most of you know, I escaped from Budapest in 1956 and never saw my family again. My wife lost both parents within the last five years. Only through the dharma have we learned to let go of all that." Ceci waited for something to follow this astonishing statement, but there was only another of those long silences Walter used for subject changes. Walter said, "At first I didn't believe it either. But what made me give it a chance was how scientific it was. This many mantras will get you that far. It's all a matter of dosage. Why shouldn't the repetition of words have a biochemical effect? All I can tell you is, it works."

Walter asked Beth to say a little about various meditation practices. Beth picked up a stack of 8 × 10 glossies; on each was a Tibetan tanka of a Buddha. Beth was even more soft-spoken than Walter, so that many of the older people had to lean forward to hear. Beth jackknifed forward, gesturing prettily, thumb and forefinger joined like a Balinese dancer as she explained what each Buddha did. The pictures were passed around.

"This is the Medicine Buddha," said Beth. "The healing Buddha. This Buddha seems to have an especially large following around here." It took all Ceci's self-restraint not to stare at her fellow Buddhists. Which ones needed healing? And what from? How ironic that now, filled with new curiosity and concern, she could not—for obvious social reasons— even turn around.

The monastery was on a mountaintop. During the break, people walked outside. It was early April, chilly. The Buddhists puffed out their cheeks and chafed their upper arms. There was a view of three states which everyone stood facing. Ceci admired it for a moment and then thought: What now? The sound of the loudest gong yet floated out over three states, and everyone filed back indoors.

Windowless, draped in red and gold silk, one whole wall occupied by a multi-tiered altar holding dozens of brass Buddhas, vases of flowers, candles, and smoldering incense holders, the temple was surprisingly convincing. Even the incense smelled venerable and antique. On one wall was a large painting of an orange-robed lama, youngish and rather plump, with the beaming, cherubic face of those fish-riding babies in popular Chinese prints. There was nothing from modern life but a large canister vacuum cleaner, propped up in the corner—useful, no doubt, for the trails of uncooked rice on the carpet.

Everyone found a pillow on the floor. When the gong sounded, Ceci closed her eyes, and, as Walter had suggested before the break, tried to meditate on her question for the Lama. But when everything settled down, the only thing she registered was her own perfume. That had been a mistake.

She imagined a company stumbling onto an indelible perfume, forced to recall it after consumer complaints, leaving thousands, including Ceci, permanently marked. This was what she was thinking about when Walter hit the gong again and said, "You'll see the Lama's appointment schedule posted in the hall. But please, come half an hour early. Remember: Tibetan time."

According to the schedule, the Lama would be seeing someone every five minutes for two hours. Ceci thought: Why, he's the Tibetan Dr. Ruth! When she saw her name at the bottom of the list—not near the bottom, but actually last—she lost all hope. She taught school. She knew how it felt to repeat yourself, day after day: Don't hit. Share. Clean up. How the Lama must wish for a tape of himself saying, "Suffering is desire."

Ceci went for a walk in the woods but felt self-conscious, as if someone were filming her. She didn't know when to start or stop or what to look at. After a few minutes she came back in and sat with the Buddhists waiting to see the Lama. They talked and talked right up to the Lama's door. But afterward, they were silent and slinked away, avoiding eye contact like moviegoers after a film that has moved them too deeply to speak.

Ceci was the last one in the lobby. She could have used this moment of solitude and peace to prepare; instead, she tortured herself wondering what airport she was in long ago when everyone else was called for a flight and the place emptied out and she realized that the plane she was about to take was a lot smaller than she'd thought. Finally Ceci heard her name, and she entered the Lama's red and gold room.

At the moment Ceci walked in, the Lama was looking at his

watch. Ceci caught him at it, and he laughed. Ceci laughed too, then was amazed to discover that she was on the verge of tears. She was just so disappointed. But what had she expected? For one thing, someone older. Only now did it occur to her that she'd had no clear picture of the Lama. Now she recognized him from his portrait, the baby-faced one, but in some new adolescent stage—gawky, thin, with the skinny head, dark-rimmed glasses, and flat-top crewcut of a guy in a fifties high-school yearbook. Some strain around the Lama's eyes convinced her that she had been correct, that right now the Lama felt just as she did by this point in the school year: drained, longing for it to be over, unable to even fake interest when another child came for help.

Ceci's mind raced wildly over everything she had to tell the Lama—an exhausting story, she saw now, endless and impossible to get through. Walter had mentioned that if they didn't have a specific question, they could simply throw themselves on the Lama's wisdom and ask for any advice that might help. Now Ceci considered doing that. But the Lama kept staring at her, his gaze so direct that Ceci could only return it in small doses.

After a while Ceci said, "My husband broke up with me at a sushi bar. We were sitting side by side. The sushi chef wasn't watching exactly, but he was there. My husband told me that he was moving to Arizona; then he ordered another cucumber salmon-skin roll. It was early for dinner. Only one table was full. Four young people, a girl and three guys—Wall Street types. I'd seen them on our way in. It had surprised me to see them so early, at such an unchic Japanese place uptown. After my husband said what he had to say, I didn't feel like talking, so we eavesdropped on their conversation about how hard it was to meet someone in the city. And I was so filled with hate for them, such bubbling-up, boundless hate. There was nothing wrong with them, they weren't obnoxious. I just hated them for being young. And I thought: Oh, I've changed. I am exactly the kind of person you tell you don't love any more, sitting shoulder to shoulder with at a sushi bar."

The Lama's expression shifted slightly, crossed some nearly imperceptible line between boredom and relief. He looked at Ceci a few seconds longer. "There is a simple meditation called the meditation of lovingkindness," he said, with hardly any accent. "Its aim is to increase your compassion. You just breathe in and out. You breathe in the suffering of those you want to help, and the suffering goes straight to your heart and destroys whatever is most self-loving and self-cherishing. And you breathe it out as white light, which goes to whoever needs it and gives them what they want."

Well, it sounded as if it couldn't hurt, but finally, what was the point? What did it have to do with Ceci or anything she had told him? How could breathing white light in and out help her, or anyone? How could her disappointment be translated into compassion, and what good was compassion without action? Don't send white light, she thought. Send money. She wanted her fifty dollars back.

The Lama said, "Just give it a ten-minute try. Ten minutes for something that's worked for three thousand years. What have you got to lose?" And Ceci thought: Why not? Really, ten minutes was nothing, nothing to lose. And what if it helped? She remembered how, in high school, she read *Franny* and Zoocy and so loved the idea of a prayer becoming part of your heartbeat. Working its biochemical magic.

The others had started without her. Only for the briefest moment did Ceci let herself feel slighted. She tiptoed into the temple and settled onto a pillow near the door. She crossed her legs and thought of what the Lama had said and started breathing. First she concentrated on that—inhaling, exhaling— then moved gingerly, testing the water, toward suffering, to- ward how much you saw if you opened your eyes on an average day in the city, how much you never saw. She conjured up stories, that restaurant for the dying, photos, terrible images of violence and death and disease until she couldn't hold her breath and breathed out, sending out health, long life, love, work—a miracle, if need be. She sent it streaming out into the world and even—this was the hardest part—to the others in the room, wishing for them whatever healing they sought in the Medicine Buddha.

She inhaled again and the images began to blur, growing brighter, coming up behind her eyelids, brilliant and warming. She felt slightly dizzy, surrounded by so much light, and yet she could still check back on herself, probing, tongue in sore tooth, for what hurt. And after some minutes it began to seem to her that her problems were, when one took the larger view, really very manageable, and rather small.

But though she kept breathing steadily, taking in and send- ing out, the light began to fade, gradually, as at dusk, when she used to read and not notice till her husband would come in and say, "You'll go blind." She breathed harder, slightly panicky now as the white light turned an odd shrimp color, then deepened to a dull blood red, and a memory stung her before she quite knew what it was.

It was something her husband once told her about his first astronomy job, as an observatory tour guide. The best part of that job, the part he never tired of, was helping the tourists see through the solar telescope, see the sun. It took quite a bit of focusing, and as the tourists struggled with it, he would look into their eyes and know exactly when they saw. Because at the moment they focused, the solar reflection flashed onto their irises: a brilliant, perfect, red disc of sun, shining at him from each eye.

W O M E N
and
C H I L D R E N
F I R S T

Gordie likes to say he can read the writing on the wall: Soon armies of upscale D.C. couples will be buying second homes in quaint Highland County, driving property values sky-high. They've already done the Blue Ridge. Janet can't quite believe that the moving finger is writing about real estate, but she knows that for Gordie prophecy means advice. Janet rents a farmhouse in

Highland and trucks in antiques which Gordie sells at American Beauty, his Georgetown shop. Gordie says that renters in Highland will soon be dinosaurs in museums; Janet should buy some failing crackerbarrel mom-and-pop store and turn it into American Beauty West.

They have just smoked a joint in Gordie's bedroom in the basement of his shop. They are sitting cross-legged on his carved four-poster bed, amid the Chinese knickknacks, the Oscar Wilde bearskin rug, the moth-eaten taxidermy Gordie says is illegal even to own, and looking through a carton of antique nursery-rhyme illustrations, the remnants of some disintegrated kids' book that someone recognized as beautiful and worth saving, and which Janet found yesterday at an estate sale in Slate Mills.

Janet turns a cardboard wheel, and beneath a cut-out window, a cow jumps over the moon. Next comes the laughing dog, then the hand-in-hand dish and spoon. Gordie says, "These are a gold mine. I can frame them—the perfect new-baby gift. Sure you don't want to steal a couple for Kevin's room?"

"Kevin?" says Janet. "Gordie, this is 'Hey Diddle Diddle.' Kevin's got Tina Turner on his wall."

"I had Tina Turner on *my* wall," Gordie says. "Well, anyway, Ike."

Janet would like to keep the page she is holding, but feels that her work gives her daily instruction in letting go. It would be easy for her to accumulate objects, to be buried beneath them. Yesterday she wondered how the elderly brother and sister who had come to supervise the estate sale, the dis-

posal of their parents' things, could sell these pictures at all—
their childhood fantasy images, a dollar for the whole box. She
kept reminding herself that there was a lesson here, that
basically they were right.

"I'll tell you something weird," she says. "Last night I
was spinning this 'Hey Diddle Diddle' wheel, just looking
at it. Kevin was upstairs asleep. After a while I heard him
come down. He said he'd had a great dream about a flying
cow."

Gordie says, "Could he have seen the picture?" and when
Janet shakes her head, he says, "You really should get this
checked out." This sounds like medical advice, which in a
way it is. Gordie has a friend at Georgetown Medical School
who told him that someone there has gotten a small grant to
study family ESP. What friend? wonders Janet. Gordie often
uses the word to mean some guy he found attractive and maybe
even had a long conversation with at a bar.

Janet says she'll ask Kevin; she knows he'll never agree.
Kevin takes it for granted that he and Janet have the same
thoughts, he can't understand why Janet gets so excited about
it. Maybe he worries that thinking like a girl means you are
one. He says that all kids and parents think alike; it comes
from living in the same house, and if it doesn't happen with
his father it's only because Will doesn't live with them but in
D.C. When Janet asks Kevin how he knows this, if he has
asked other kids, he says, "Are you crazy?" What, then, would
he think of scientists getting grants to ask other parents and
kids? He'd think it was weird; and worse, he'd know that it
would involve every kind of attention he hates.

Just before Janet leaves Georgetown, Gordie asks if she doesn't at least want to keep the cow jumping over the moon. Janet makes a little sweep with her hand. "Gordie," she says, "I'm just a conduit. Hear the wind blowing through?"

On the drive back to Monterey, Janet keeps looking in her rear-view mirror, imagining Gordie's armies, the convoys of house-hunting Volvos and Saabs bearing down on her. She feels nearly queasy with secret knowledge, as if she alone sees the enemy massing on the Eastern front. Nearly home, she stops for a couple of hitchhikers—local characters, old hippies Kevin refers to as Mr. Time Travel and his wife. They are often on the road; Janet has picked them up a few times before and does so again today because Mrs. Time Travel appears to be hugely pregnant. When the man helps his wife into the cab of the truck, Janet smells patchouli. The woman was overweight to begin with, but her husband is very bony. It averages out; they fit fairly comfortably on the front seat. As Janet drives them into Staunton, Mr. Time Travel tells her how their welfare worker is threatening to cut them off if his wife doesn't get to a doctor. He talks very softly about the horrors of hospital birth—women trussed up and drugged, bright lights shining in babies' eyes—and every time he says "trussed up" Janet feels his wife flinch.

Something about this makes Janet determined to bring Kevin in for the ESP experiments. Maybe it's the impulse to distinguish herself from these dinosaurs, to identify as the modern, if downwardly mobile, former wife of a surgeon and the mother of a perfectly healthy hospital-born kid. Partly, she just longs for something new. When she and Will split up and she found this way to live out here and make money, she'd thought that the rest of her life would be a treasure hunt. The auctions, the sales, checking the local obits—how quickly it all came to seem like a job. It's got so her heart sinks at the sight of another beautiful oak hutch. Also, she wonders if this new desire to be a famous ESP guinea pig is just that old dream of specialness, of celebrity and revenge: mind-reading mom and kid amazing talk-show hosts, written up by Oliver Sacks so even Will can read it.

She wants to just do it—just go there for the experiments, not argue—so that night at dinner she tells Kevin that if he comes with her, no questions asked, he can have a new base-ball mitt and two computer games.

"Medical school?" Kevin says.

"Trust me," says Janet, and they both smile, because this is Kevin's expression. "No doctors," she says. "Looking at pictures. ESP experiments. That kind of thing. Okay, listen. They'll pay us ten dollars an hour. You get to keep the money."

"Ten dollars an hour?" he repeats, and when Janet nods, he says, "That and the ant farm." Lately he has been asking for an ant farm; she should have thought of that right away. Where did he hear about ant farms? And where in the world do you get one? Tracking down items from science-museum shops is not the kind of thing either she or Will does well, especially not now, with Will spending every free minute with his new girlfriend. She thinks there's some rigamarole about getting the ants. And the way Kevin takes care of things, there's a good chance that dirt, broken glass and a million ants will wind up on his bedroom floor. Still it seems like something you'd want to buy your kid, feel better about than computer games.

"Okay, the ant farm," she says.

Janet makes an appointment at the medical school for a Wednesday; she tells Kevin he'll learn as much as he would have from two days at school. At one time he liked missing school, no matter what. But now he's clearly torn, and on the day of the appointment, Janet feels so guilty that she stops, without his even asking, for take-out McDonald's breakfast. As they merge with the stream of trucks on Route 74, she says, "In a few years, you'll be driving. It seems impossible—you were just this little baby."

After a long silence, Kevin says, "Do you have to catch the ants, or can you just buy them somewhere?"

"I don't know," Janet says. "I'll find out."

And that's it for conversation. For most of the drive, Kevin stares out the window. Glancing over at him, Janet thinks how soon he will be a teenager; now he is right on the edge. It occurs to her that being so handsome may make it easier for him, but she can't tell him this; it is already too late.

She pulls into the Park 'n Ride lot, where Gordie is waiting. His metal-flake emerald '56 Buick gleams like a giant eight-cylinder scarab. Janet is glad to see him, glad that he offered to close the store and come with them. She loves riding in Gordie's car: everyone turns to look at you as you sink into the deep sofa-like seats and breathe in the stuffy, indescribable smell of your childhood. Gordie said he wanted to expedite their trip, to free their minds for higher things, but Janet suspects that he'd like to run into his friend at the medical school. She can't blame him. At the back of her mind is the fact that where they're going isn't far from Will's office. She imagines meeting him, imagines the look on his face, that sympathetic doctor's look of perplexity and concern.

The waiting room reminds her of an expensive obstetrician's—in fact, of the office of the old man Will knew who delivered Kevin for free. It's smaller, of course, and empty, but even so, Janet has that waiting-room self-consciousness as she sits between Kevin with his punky baseball cap pulled over his eyes and Gordie with his ginger moustache and leather bomber jacket; as if there were anyone there to approve, she feels proud to be sitting between them. Kevin likes Gordie, though he spends too much time with his dad and Will's doctor-intellectual friends to give Gordie much credit as a full-scale human adult. Gordie has brought Kevin treasures— special marbles, a rooster-shaped tin bank, a revolving lamp with a scene of Niagara Falls—which Kevin seems to like but leaves all over his room.

After a while, a receptionist calls Janet and Kevin. Gordie says, "Adiós and good luck. If I'm not here, I'm taking a walk, I'll be back." The receptionist, a barrel-like young woman, takes off down the scratchy-industrial-carpeted hall; Janet and Kevin fly after her, and so have to brake sharply when she motions them through an office door.

Inside, a woman sits behind the desk, a man in the chair beside her. The woman is wearing a lab coat. Janet wonders why she needs it; she'd always thought lab coats were to guard against spraying mouse blood. The man and the woman stand to shake hands. They are both about Janet's age, a fact which horrifies and convinces her that she shouldn't have come. She feels humiliated, as if being on the opposite side of this scientific investigation is an admission of failure in life.

The woman introduces herself as Dr. Wilmot. She is tall, a light-skinned black woman with huge, stylish eyeglasses, a clear, lively smile, and unruly, half-straight hair. She introduces the man as Dr. Becker, and he laughs and says, "Eric." He is good-looking in that clean, academic way that can make jeans and rolled shirt sleeves look like a lab coat: not clinical, exactly, just terribly pressed and neat. When Eric shakes Janet's hand, he smiles and looks at her closely. She focuses on a postcard tacked to the corkboard on the wall behind him—a vintage anthropological photo of two pygmy women playing ping-pong.

Dr. Wilmot says she'd like to say a few things about the study. She says they are lucky, that there's really no money around for this kind of project these days. She says the experiment is simply the classic model: they'll be put in separate rooms and asked to look at pictures. She asks if they have any questions. Janet can't think of one. Kevin looks too bored to speak.

They leave Dr. Wilmot's office and walk awkwardly down the hall; no one knows who to walk with. After a while they reach two open doors. Dr. Wilmot motions Janet and Eric into one room, she and Kevin take the other. Janet is glad that it's not the other way round. She wonders if this arrangement is accidental or if research has discovered that ESP gets sharper around a slight sexual buzz.

As Kevin disappears through the door, Dr. Wilmot smiles encouragingly, but with a certain strain, so that it comes out almost a leer. Janet feels strange, as if she's involving her child in something scandalous, like some Victorian father introducing his son to the local bordello.

The room Eric takes her into is dimly lit, bare but for two wooden chairs and a wooden table, rather like the set of a low-budget avant-garde play. On the table is a stack of cards, face down, also a clipboard and pen. Eric picks up the clipboard and says he is sorry, he has to take a history. Again Janet has a flash of the obstetrician's, more panicky now, but at least he doesn't ask when she got chicken pox or her first period, facts she's long since forgotten and so always has to reinvent. He asks about traumatic childhood illnesses or experiences, hers or Kevin's. Janet says, "Normal, normal, normal." Finally he asks, "When was the first time you sensed some special connection with your son?"

"Special connection?" she says.

Eric's gesture takes in the room. "You know," he says.

"Do you have kids?" asks Janet.

Eric jumps slightly, then says, "Three. They live with their mother. I get them alternate weekends." He says this with some bewilderment, as if he hasn't yet figured out why this should be. Janet finds it encouraging, and goes back to considering his question. Special connection? There was that night just before she went into labor, when the baby's kicking woke her up, and she knew—she just knew—he was miserable, he didn't want to be born. But maybe mentioning this will label her right from the start as an unreliable subject.

So she tells him about the first incident actually witnessed by bona-fide-scientist Will. "This is a crazy story," she says. Eric moves his chair nearer hers. "I was breaking up with my husband. At that time I thought I'd stay in D.C. For Kevin. Will was helping me find an apartment. The first place we saw was full of eyeballs. Everywhere—the kitchen counter, the toilet tank, every surface was covered with plasticene eyeballs. It turned out that the woman who lived there made models for a medical supply house and she'd gotten a big order. My husband is a doctor, he'd used models like that in medical school, so they had lots to talk about. I knew I couldn't live there, even though she was taking the eyeballs with her, and on the way home my husband and I had a fight, because otherwise it was a perfectly good apartment, and why was I being so squeamish? We picked Kevin up at my friend's. And she was in a bad mood because her kid was Kevin's age and couldn't draw a straight line and Kevin had spent the whole afternoon drawing these perfect eyeballs."

"Wow," Eric says. "Is that really true?"

"Every word," says Janet, though she's left out the fact that the eyeball-apartment woman was young and pretty.

"How did your husband feel about it?" Eric asks.

"He hated it. He acted like I did it on purpose, coached Kevin. I stopped telling him when things like that happened, but sometimes, when they happened in front of him, he used to say he felt like an actor in one of those disaster movies with the Titanic sinking and everyone yelling, 'Women and children first!' except that his wife and kid had already gone and left him standing on deck, watching their lifeboat float off."

Janet realizes she has never even told Gordie about Will saying this. She only mentioned it once, drunk, at a D.C. party. Someone was talking about the actual Titanic, and she stopped the whole conversation by quoting Will. There was a terrible silence, till finally some lefty lawyer type said something lame and solemn—meant, nonetheless, as a halfhearted come-on— about the whole male sex being stuck on a sinking ship.

"I used to feel awful when he'd say that," Janet says. "I'd think: Hey, he's a doctor, he has enough in his life without envying me and Kevin. But I don't know. I guess he felt left out; I guess everybody wants everything."

Janet pauses, slightly embarrassed and pleased that saying "everybody wants everything" may have made her sound like a greedy slave of appetite. She doubts that it's even true. One night last fall, when Kevin was in D.C., Janet went home with a man—a candlemaker—she met at a Charlottesville crafts fair. After a while, he showed her into his bedroom; he'd lit mush- room candles all over. Though touched by his attempt at romance, she was appalled by those hideous glowing mush- rooms, and she couldn't go through with it; she excused herself and left.

What she wants to tell Eric is how, in the end, Will was really the prescient one. Because, finally, wasn't he right? Janet and Kevin in one boat, Will in another, an ocean—all right, a highway—between them. Sometimes it astonishes her that her strongest—her only—connection is with a child. It's common enough, she knows, just not what she expected. And now, when she imagines those disaster films, it's the women's faces she sees, the looks on their faces as they climb down into the boats: fear mixed with amazement that when the order came, they so readily, so instinctively complied. But saying this might make her life with Kevin sound impenetrable, closed-off, full-up. It's why, she sometimes thinks, she's so adamant about not accumulating lots of stuff. What man wouldn't hesitate in the doorway of a house where a woman and child live surrounded by perfect antiques?

Eric says, "Was that part of what came between you?"

"The tiniest part," she says. Then they both fall silent. Janet remembers a magazine article which claimed that one sign of sexual interest is the reflected gesture: she picks up a glass, he picks up a glass, he crosses his legs, so does she. She hopes that shared silence counts. She thinks about Kevin and Dr. Wilmot on the other side of the wall: if she's been taking his medical history, they would have finished long ago. Then a red darkroom light blinks on the wall, and Eric gives her the stack of cards and says, "Here's the story. Simple geometric images—triangles, squares. We're trying to eliminate the variables."

Janet is disappointed: the experiments she's read about used images like camels in the desert, the Alamo, rockets in outer space. Though maybe that's why they never got conclusive results. Eric explains that in the first round Kevin will send, Janet receive. He tells Janet to close her eyes and concentrate, and call out whatever comes to mind. Janet imagines triangles, squares. They all seem equally likely. None of them flash on and off or in any way signal her as beaming from Kevin's brain.

Her only thoughts are of Eric, how conscious she is of him awaiting her answer; she desperately wants to do well. She thinks: Everything is backwards. Here she is, going through this with her kid, and the only telepathy she cares about is with the guy running the test. It's hopelessly distracting, but when it's her turn, sending seems somewhat easier. She fixes her eyes on the triangle and wonders if Kevin will blame her for making him do yet another boring thing that she'd thought would be fun.

Finally Eric says, "Well, that's it." They look at each other a moment too long. Janet looks away. There's some complicated timing here, much more finely tuned than who picks up the wine glass first. They leave the room together; Dr. Wilmot and Kevin are already in the hall. When Kevin pouts, as he's doing now, he looks like a much younger kid. Janet has a moment of hating herself for the disloyalty of dragging Kevin here, making him sit through this, and, on top of all that, wishing he would act friendlier for some guy she's just met.

Dr. Wilmot asks if Janet and Kevin will bear with them for just a few more minutes in the waiting room. Janet and Eric exchange a quick heavy look, embarrassingly reminiscent of suburban-adultery movies. Janet says, "No problem."

Gordie glances up when they enter, and for a moment Janet wonders what he's doing there. He looks so out of context, so far from the Victorian burgundy-reds of his bedroom. It reduces him, the way baseball stars look smaller when you see them in business suits on the evening news. "How was it?" he says.

"Tons of fun," says Kevin. Janet is about to ask Gordie if he met up with his friend when Dr. Wilmot and Eric walk in.

"Eric," says Gordie.

Eric looks a little blankly at Gordie, then says, "Oh, hi."

"You guys know each other?" says Janet. Eric looks from Janet to Gordie, somehow managing to pay them both that same serious attention Janet felt from him back in the room.

Well, you can never tell. Janet reminds herself not to jump to conclusions. Eric might not even be gay; Gordie is always developing these sudden impossible crushes.

Dr. Wilmot tells them that the final results aren't in yet but right now the quick match-ups indicate an unusually high score, at least in one direction—Janet sending, Kevin receiving. Janet feels wronged: in fact she knows Kevin's thoughts as often as he knows hers. She has a childish desire to say that it's Eric's fault for ruining her concentration. But she can only smile lamely as Dr. Wilmot says she'll be in touch with them about follow-up tests, and they can expect payment shortly. "The check's in the mail," she says, and they all laugh. Everyone says goodbye and shakes hands except Kevin, who stands in the doorway, impatiently rolling his eyes.

On the way to the car, Kevin walks ahead. "Watch out, it's a parking lot," calls Janet.

Gordie says, "What did you think about Eric?"

"Very cute," says Janet.

"No," says Gordie. "I mean, you're the one with ESP. Do you think he's gay?"

Janet should be cheered by this. Maybe there is some basis to whatever she felt in that room—maybe Eric will call, maybe anything else is in Gordie's mind. Then she remembers how Eric looked at them, both of them. She thinks: Maybe Eric is just your basic compulsive seducer. Suddenly she feels exhausted. It occurs to her that if you heard what was said in any hospital parking lot on any average day, you would hear lots of bad news. And suddenly she can't bring herself to give Gordie one bit more. "Yes," she says. "I do. He couldn't keep his eyes off you."

"Really?" says Gordie.

"Trust me," says Janet.

They find Kevin sitting on the hood of Gordie's car, his long legs dangling. He gets in the back, and Janet slides in beside Gordie.

A block from the hospital, Gordie stops at a crosswalk and waves some pedestrians across—an Italian or Hispanic family, formally dressed, walking slowly so as to wait for a little girl in a white communion dress who is limping, straggling behind, stopping every few minutes to pop her white pump off her heel and lift her foot and examine it. Even from the car, Janet can see the angry blister on the girl's heel. Suddenly she wishes Will were there—or maybe not Will, just someone, a husband or lover she trusted to know what she couldn't begin to say about that little girl, that white dress, that blister.

From the back seat, Kevin says, "What's the point of having ESP if you can't tell when girls like you?"

He sounds furious, and this surprises Janet more than what he has said, or that he should have said it at all. There's a silence. Finally Gordie says, "Good question."

Janet knows she could blow the moment completely by asking, "Like who? Like which girls?" She takes a deep breath before she says, "Well, you can. A lot of times you can. You just learn how, that's all."

"How?" Kevin says.

"Take your father," Janet says. "We were eating in a restaurant with these friends who were introducing us—"

"Who?" asks Kevin.

"You didn't know them," she says. "They moved when you were little. They had a kid they let run everything. He even got to pick the restaurant, so we ate at a diner he liked because it had mirrored walls. But that night he didn't care about the walls. He wouldn't sit in his chair; he ran around, getting under the waitresses' feet, and our friends kept having to jump up and drag him back. Each time, one of them would say, 'You go, I went last time,' so things were a little tense. From time to time they'd tease your dad about having a kid, having to do what they were doing; I guess he had a reputation for not liking kids. Finally he called the kid over and sat him down between us—we were on the same side of the booth. He cut the kid's hamburger up for him, in little pieces, and the kid was so surprised that he shut up and ate his whole meal. Our friends didn't say a word. They must have been wondering what had come over your dad. But I knew he was doing it for me, to show me he was the kind of guy who could be nice to kids."

"Right," says Kevin. Right about what? Janet wonders, but lets it go. Will was always nice to Kevin, or, anyway, an acceptable balance of nice and not nice, no more or less nice then she was. Anyway, she doesn't want to think about that, she just wants to sit and remember that night in the restaurant—not the noisy kid, the bickering parents, but this: how Will's hands shook as he sawed away at that burger, and how she had thought, Here was a surgeon, a man with steady hands, and look, look, what power she had.

"Aren't you ever wrong?" Kevin says.

Gordie says, "Not about that. If there's one thing your Mom's psychic about, it's that."

Janet looks out the window. They're almost at the Park 'n Ride where she's left the truck; she wishes she'd used the bathroom in the medical school. Now there are only gas stations from here on out. She is frightened of public bathrooms and mostly tries not to use them. The only time they didn't scare her were when she was pregnant with Kevin. Then nothing bothered her, not the grime or the buzzing flourescent lights or the empty shine of the tiles, the pin-scratched initials, the rust like drops of blood on skin. Nothing frightened her then. She had company.

They say goodbye to Gordie and drive off. A few miles past the beltway, Kevin says, "Could you pull over somewhere?"

Janet drives onto the shoulder and Kevin climbs down from the truck. As Kevin heads towards the edge of the woods, he keeps stopping, crouching down. It takes her a while to figure out: he's looking for ants. She watches till he's hidden by trees, and she can no longer see him.

It seems like a long time till he reappears, and though she tells herself that nothing could have happened, she is beginning to get anxious when she spots his blue baseball cap. Emerging from the woods, he waves at her—a broad, enthusiastic wave, as if from miles away.

OTHER

LIVES

Climbing up with a handful of star decals to paste on the bathroom ceiling, Claire sees a suspect-looking shampoo bottle on the cluttered top shelf. When she opens it, the whole room smells like a subway corridor where bums have been pissing for generations. She thinks back a few days to when Miranda and Poppy were playing in here with the door shut. She puts down the stars and yells for the girls with such urgency they come running before she's finished emptying it into the sink.

From the doorway, Poppy and her best friend Miranda look at Claire, then at each other. "Mom," says Poppy, "you threw it out?"

Claire wants to ask why they're saving their urine in bottles. But sitting on the edge of the tub has lowered her eye level and she's struck speechless by the beauty of their kneecaps, their long suntanned legs. How strong and shaky and elegant they are. Like newborn giraffes. By now she can't bring herself to ask, so she tells them not to do it again and is left with the rest of the morning to wonder what they had in mind.

She thinks it has something to do with alchemy and with faith, with those moments when children are playing with such pure concentration that anything is possible and the rest of the world drops away and becomes no more real than one of their 3-D Viewmaster slides. She remembers when she was Poppy's age, playing with her own best friend Evelyn. Evelyn's father had been dead several years, but his medical office in a separate wing of their house was untouched, as if office hours might begin any minute. In his chilly consulting room, smelling of carpet dust and furniture polish and, more faintly, of gauze and sterilizing pans, Claire and Evelyn played their peculiar version of doctor. Claire would come in, and from behind the desk Evelyn would give her some imaginary pills. Then Claire would fall down dead and Evelyn would kneel and listen to her heart and say, "I'm sorry, it's too late."

But what Claire remembers best is the framed engraving on Evelyn's father's desk. It was one of those trompe l'oeil pieces you see sometimes in cheap art stores. From one angle, it looked like two Gibson girls at a table sipping ice cream sodas through straws. From another, it looked like a skull. Years later, when Claire learned that Evelyn's father had actually died in jail where he'd been sent for performing illegal abortions, she'd thought: What an odd picture to have on an abortionist's desk. But at the time, it had just seemed marvelous. She used to unfocus her eyes and tilt her head so that it flipped back and forth. Skull, ladies. Skull, ladies. Skull.

Dottie's new hairdo, a wide corolla of pale blond curls, makes her look even more like a sunflower—spindly, graceful, rather precariously balanced. At one, when Dottie comes to pick up Miranda, Claire decides not to tell her about the shampoo bottle.

Lately, Dottie's had her mind on higher things. For the past few months, she's been driving down to the New Consciousness Academy in Bennington where she takes courses with titles like "Listening to the Inner Silence" and "Weeds for Your Needs." Claire blames this on one of Dottie's friends, an electrician named Jeanette. Once at a party, Claire overheard Jeanette telling someone how she and her boyfriend practice birth control based on lunar astrology and massive doses of wintergreen tea.

"Coffee?" says Claire tentatively. It's hard to keep track of what substances Dottie's given up. Sometimes, most often in winter, when Joey and Raymond are working and the girls are at school, Dottie and Claire get together for lunch. Walking into Dottie's house and smelling woodsmoke and wine and fresh-baked bread, seeing the table set with blue bowls and hothouse anemones and a soup thick with sausage, potatoes, tomatoes put up from the fall, Claire used to feel that she must be living her whole life right. All summer she's been praying that Dottie won't give up meat.

Dottie says, "Have you got any herbal tea?" and Claire says, "Are you kidding?" "All right, coffee," says Dottie. "Just this once."

As Claire pours the coffee, Dottie fishes around in her enormous parachute-silk purse. Recently Dottie's been bringing Claire reading material. She'd started off with Krishnamurti, Rajneesh, the songs of Milarepa. Claire tried, but she just couldn't; she'd returned them unread. A few weeks back, she'd brought something by Dashiell Hammett about a man named Flitcraft who's walking to lunch one day and a beam falls down from a construction site and just misses him, and he just keeps walking and never goes to his job or back to his wife and family again.

When Claire read that, she wanted to call Dottie up and make her promise not to do something similar. But she didn't. The last time she and Dottie discussed the Academy, Dottie described a technique she'd learned for closing her eyes and pressing on her eyelids just hard enough to see thousands of pinpricks of light. Each one of those dots represents a past life, and if you know how to look, you can see it. In this way, Dottie learned that she'd spent a former life as a footsoldier in Napoleon's army on the killing march to Moscow. That's why she so hates the cold. Somehow Claire hadn't known that Dottie hated the winter, but really, it follows: a half-starved, half-frozen soldier cooking inspired sausage soup three lives later.

"I meant to bring you a book," says Dottie. Then she says, "A crazy thing happened this morning. I was working in front of the house, digging up those irises by the side of the road so I could divide them. I didn't hear anything but I must have had a sense because I turned around and there was this old lady—coiffed, polyestered, dressed for church, it looked like. She told me she'd come over from Montpelier with some friends for a picnic and got separated. Now she was lost and so upset.

"I said, 'Well, okay, I'll drive you back to Montpelier.' We got as far as Barre when suddenly her whole story started coming apart, and I realized: She hadn't been in Montpelier for twenty years. She was from the Good Shepherd House, that old folks' home up the road from us. I drove her back to the Good Shepherd—what else could I do? The manager thanked me, he was very embarrassed she'd escaped. Then just as I was pulling out, the old lady pointed up at the sky and gave me the most hateful triumphant smile, and I looked up through the windshield and there was this flock of geese heading south." Dottie catches her breath, then says, "You know what? It's August. I'd forgotten."

What Claire can't quite forget is that years ago, the first time she and Joey met Dottie and Raymond, afterward Joey said, "They don't call her 'dotty' for nothing." It took them both a while to see that what looked at first like dottiness was really an overflow of the same generosity which makes Dottie cook elegant, warming meals and drive senile old ladies fifty miles out of her way to Montpelier. On Tuesdays and Thursdays, when Dottie goes down to the Academy, she's a volunteer chauffeur service, picking up classmates—including Jeanette the electrician—from all over central Vermont. Even Joey's come around to liking her, though Claire's noticed that he's usually someplace else when Dottie's around.

Now he's in the garden, tying up some tomatoes that fell last night in the wind. Finding them this morning—perfect red tomatoes smashed on top of each other—had sent her straight to the bathroom with her handful of star decals. That's the difference between me and Joey, Claire thinks. Thank God there's someone to save what's left of the vines.

Joey doesn't see Claire watching him but Dottie does and starts to flutter, as if she's overstayed. She calls up to Miranda, and just when it begins to seem as if they might not have heard, the girls drag themselves downstairs.

"Why does Miranda have to go?" says Poppy.

"Because it's fifteen miles and Miranda's mom isn't driving fifteen miles back and forth all day," says Claire.

"But I don't want to go," says Miranda.

They stand there, deadlocked, until Poppy says, "I've got an idea. I'll go home with Miranda and tonight her mom and dad can come to dinner and bring us both back and then Miranda can sleep over."

"That's fine with me," says Claire.

"Are you sure?" says Dottie.

Claire's sure. As Dottie leans down to kiss her goodbye, Claire thinks once more of sunflowers, specifically of the ones she and Joey and Poppy plant every summer on a steep slope so you can stand underneath and look up and the sunflowers look forty feet tall.

·   ·   ·

Washing his hands at the sink, Joey says, "One day she's going to show up in saffron robes with a begging bowl and her hair shaved down to one skanky topknot and then what?"

Claire thinks: Well, then we'll cook up some gluey brown rice and put a big glob in Dottie's bowl. But this sounds like something they'd say at the New Consciousness Academy, some dreadful homily about adaptation and making do. All she can think of is, "I cried because I had no shoes until I met a man who had no feet," and that's not it.

One night, not long after Dottie started attending the Academy, they were all sitting outside and Dottie looked up and said, "Sometimes I feel as if my whole life is that last minute of the planetarium show when they start showing off— that is, showing off what their projector can do—and the moon and planets and stars and even those distant galaxies begin spinning like crazy while they tell you the coming attractions and what time the next show begins. I just want to find someplace where it's not rushing past me so fast. Or where, if it is, I don't care."

"I hope you find it," Joey said. "I really do." Later that night, he told Claire that he knew what Dottie meant. "Still," he said, "it was creepy. The whole conversation was like talking to someone who still thinks *El Topo* is the greatest movie ever made."

Joey had gone through his own spiritual phase: acid, Castaneda, long Sunday afternoons in front of the tankas in the Staten Island Tibetan museum. All this was before he met Claire. He feels that his having grown out of it fifteen years ago gives him the right to criticize. Though actually, he's not mocking Dottie so much as protecting her husband Raymond, his best friend. Remote as the possibility seems, no one wants Dottie to follow in Flitcraft's footsteps.

Now Claire says, "I don't think she'd get her hair permed if she was planning to shave it." Then she steels herself, and in the tone of someone expecting bad news asks if any tomatoes are left. Joey says, "We'll be up to our ears in tomatoes," and Claire thinks: He'd say that no matter what.

One thing she loves about Joey is his optimism. If he's ever discontent, she doesn't know it. Once he'd wanted to be on stage, then he'd worked for a while as a landscaper, now he's a junior-high science teacher—a job which he says requires the combined talents of an actor and a gardener. His real passion is for the names of things: trees, animals, stars. But he's not one of those people who use such knowledge to make you feel small. It's why he's a popular teacher and why Poppy so loves to take walks with him, naming the wildflowers in the fields. Claire knows how rare it is for children to want to learn anything from their parents.

When Claire met Joey, she'd just moved up to Vermont with a semi-alcoholic, independently wealthy photographer named Dell. Dell hired Joey to clear a half acre around their cabin so they could have a garden and lawn. Upstairs there's a photo Dell took of them at the time and later sent as a wedding present to prove there were no hard feelings. It shows Claire and Joey leaning against Joey's rented backhoe; an uprooted acacia tree is spilling out of the bucket. Joey and Claire look cocky and hard in the face, like teenage killers, Charlie Starkweather and his girl. Claire can hardly remember Dell's face. He always had something in front of it—a can of beer, a camera. If he had only put it down and looked, he'd have seen what was going on. Anyone would have. In the photo, it's early spring, the woods are full of musical names: trillium, marsh marigold, jack-in-the-pulpit.

On the day they learned Claire was pregnant and went straight from the doctor's to the marriage license bureau in Burlington, Joey pulled off the road on the way home and took Claire's face in his hands and told her which animals mated for life. Whooping cranes, snow geese, macaws, she's forgotten the rest. Now they no longer talk this way, or maybe it goes without saying. Claire's stopped imagining other lives; if she could, she'd live this one forever. Though she knows it's supposed to be dangerous to get too comfortable, she feels it would take a catastrophe to tear the weave of their daily routine. They've weathered arguments, and those treacherous, tense, dull periods when they sneak past each other as if they're in constant danger of sneezing in each other's faces. Claire knows to hold on and wait for the day when what interests her most is what Joey will have to say about it.

Some things get better. Claire used to hate thinking about the lovers they'd had before; now all that seems as indistinct as Dell's face. Though they've had eight years to get used to the fact of Poppy's existence, they're still susceptible to attacks of amazement that they've created a new human being. And often when they're doing something together—cooking, gardening, making love—Claire comes as close as she ever has to those moments of pure alchemy, that communion Poppy and Miranda must share if they're storing their pee in bottles.

Soon they'll get up and mix some marinade for the chickens they'll grill outside later for Dottie and Raymond. But now Joey pours himself some coffee and they sit at the table, not talking. It is precisely the silence they used to dream of when Poppy was little and just having her around was like always having the bath water running or something about to boil over on the stove.

First the back doors fly open and the girls jump out of the car and run up to Poppy's room. Then Dottie gets out, then Raymond. From the beginning, Raymond's reminded Claire of the tin woodsman in The Wizard of Oz, and often he'll stop in the middle of things as if waiting for someone to come along with the oil can. He goes around to the trunk and takes out a tripod and something wrapped in a blanket which looks at first like a rifle and turns out to be a telescope.

"Guess what!" When Raymond shouts like that, you can see how snaggletoothed he is. "There's a meteor shower tonight. The largest concentration of shooting stars all year."

The telescope is one of the toys Raymond's bought since his paintings started selling. Raymond's success surprises them all, including Raymond. His last two shows were large paintings of garden vegetables with skinny legs and big feet in familiar dance situations. It still surprises Claire that the New York art world would open its heart—would have a heart to open—to work bordering on the cartoonish and sentimental. But there's something undeniably mysterious and moving about those black daikon radishes doing the tango, those little cauliflowers in pink tutus on point before an audience of sleek and rather parental-looking green peppers. And there's no arguing with Raymond's draftmanship or the luminosity of his color; it's as if Memling lived through the sixties and took too many drugs. What's less surprising is that there are so many rich people who for one reason or another want to eat breakfast beneath a painting of dancing vegetables.

Claire has a crush on Raymond; at least that's what she thinks it is. It's not especially intense or very troublesome; it's been going on a long time and she doesn't expect it to change. If anything did change, it would probably disappear. She doesn't want to live with Raymond, and now, as always when he hugs her hello, their bones grate; it's not particularly sexual.

She just likes him, that's all. When it's Raymond coming to dinner, she cooks and dresses with a little more care than she otherwise might, and spends the day remembering things to tell him which she promptly forgets. Of course, she's excited when Dottie, or anyone, is coming over. The difference is, with Dottie, Claire enjoys her food. With Raymond, she often forgets to eat.

Barbecued chicken, tomatoes with basil and mozzarella, pasta with chanterelles Joey's found in the woods—it all goes right by her. Luckily, everyone else is eating, the girls trekking back and forth from the table to the TV. The television noise makes it hard to talk. It's like family dinner, they can just eat. Anyway, conversation's been strained since Dottie started at the Academy. Claire fears that Joey might make some semi-sarcastic remark which will hurt Raymond more than Dottie. Raymond's protective of her; they seem mated for life. It's occurred to them all that Dottie is the original dancing vege-table.

What does get said is that the meteor shower isn't supposed to pick up till around midnight. But they'll set up the telescope earlier so the girls can have a look before they're too tired to see.

Joey and Raymond and the girls go outside while Dottie and Claire put the dishes in the sink. Claire asks if Poppy was any trouble that afternoon and Dottie says, "Oh, no. They played in the bathroom so quiet, I had to keep yelling up to make sure they were breathing. Later they told me they'd been making vanishing cream from that liquidy soap at the bottom of the soap dish. I said, you're eight years old, what do you need with vanishing cream? They said, to vanish. I told them they'd better not use it till they had something to bring them back from wherever they vanished to, and they said, yeah, they'd already thought of that."

"Where did they *hear* about vanishing cream?" says Claire. She feels she ought to tell Dottie—feels disloyal for not telling her—to watch for suspicious-looking shampoo bottles on the upper shelves. But she doesn't. It's almost as if she's saving it for something.

"Speaking of vanishing," says Dottie. She hands Claire the book she'd forgotten that afternoon. It's Calvino's *The Baron in the Trees*. Claire's read it before, and it seems like the right moment to ask, so she says, "Does this mean that you're going to get up from the table one night and climb up in the trees and never come down again?"

Dottie just looks at her. "Me in the trees?" she says. "With my allergies?"

They're amazed by how dark it is when they go outside. "I told you," says Dottie. "It's August."

The grass is damp and cool against their ankles as they walk across the lawn to where Miranda and Poppy are taking turns at the telescope. "Daddy," Claire hears Poppy say, "what's that?"

Joey crouches down and looks over her shoulder. Claire wonders what they see. Scorpio? Andromeda? Orion? Joey's told her a thousand times but she can never remember what's in the sky when.

Before Joey can answer, Raymond pulls Poppy away from the telescope and kneels and puts one arm around her and the other around Miranda. "That one?" he says, pointing. "That one's the Bad Baby. And it's lying in the Big Bassinet."

"Where?" cry the girls, and then they say, "Yes, I see!"

"And that one there's the Celestial Dog Dish. And that"— he traces his finger in a wavy circle—"is the Silver Dollar Pancake."

"What's that one?" says Miranda.

"Remember *Superman II*?" Raymond's the one who takes the girls to movies no one else wants to see. "That's what's left of the villains after they get turned to glass and smashed to smithereens."

"Oh, no," say the girls, and hide their faces against Raymond's long legs.

Claire's tensed, as if Raymond's infringed on Joey's right to name things, or worse, is making fun of him. But Joey's laughing, he likes Raymond's names as much as the real ones. Claire steps up to the telescope and aims it at the thin crescent moon, at that landscape of chalk mountains and craters like just-burst bubbles. But all she sees is the same flat white she can see with her naked eye. Something's wrong with the telescope, or with her. The feeling she gets reminds her of waking up knowing the day's already gone wrong but not yet why, of mornings when Poppy's been sick in the night, or last summer when Joey's mother was dying.

By now the others are all lying on the hillside looking for shooting stars. There aren't any, not yet. Claire wonders if Dottie is listening to the inner silence, or thinking of past lives; if Raymond is inventing more constellations. She can't imagine what Joey's thinking. She herself can't get her mind off Jeanette the electrician and her boyfriend, drinking wintergreen tea and checking that sliver of moon to see if this is a safe night for love.

On the way in, Joey says, "Lying out there, I remembered this magazine article I read years ago, about Jean Genet at the '68 Democratic convention in Chicago. The whole time, he kept staring at the dashboard of the car they were driving him in. And afterwards, when they asked him what he thought about the riots, the beatings and so forth, he just shrugged and said, 'What can you expect from a country that would make a car named Galaxy?' "

Over coffee, the conversation degenerates into stories they've told before, tales of how the children tyrannize and abuse them, have kept them prisoner in their own homes for years at a time. The reason they can talk like this is that they all know: the children are the light of their lives. A good part of why they stay here is that Vermont seems like an easy place to raise kids. Even their children have visionary names: Poppy, Miranda. O brave new world!

When Claire first moved here with Dell, she commuted to New York, where she was working as a freelance costume designer. She likes to tell people that the high point of her career was making a holster and fringed vest and chaps for a chicken to wear on *Hee Haw*. Later she got to see it on TV, the chicken panicky and humiliated in its cowboy suit, flapping in circles while Grandpa Jones fired blanks at its feet and yelled, "Dance!" Soon it will be Halloween and Claire will sew Poppy a costume. So far she's been a jar of peanut butter, an anteater with pockets full of velveteen ants, Rapunzel. Last fall Claire made her a caterpillar suit with a back that unzipped and reversed out into butterfly wings. Poppy's already told her that this year she wants to be new wave, so all Claire will have to do is rip up a T-shirt and buy tights and wraparound shades and blue spray-on washable hair dye.

Dottie is telling about the girls making vanishing cream when Joey pretends to hear something in the garden and excuses himself and goes out. Dottie says she wants to stay up for the meteor shower but is feeling tired so she'll lie down awhile on the living-room couch.

Claire and Raymond are left alone at the table. It takes them so long to start talking, Claire's glad her crush on Raymond will never be anything more; if they had to spend a day in each other's company, they'd run out of things to say. Still, it's exciting. Raymond seems nervous, too.

Finally he asks how her day was, and Claire's surprised to hear herself say, "Pretty awful." She hadn't meant to complain, nor had she thought her day was so awful. Now she thinks maybe it was. "Nothing really," she says. "One little thing after another. Have you ever had days when you pick up a pen and the phone rings and when you get off, you can't find the pen?"

"Me?" says Raymond. "I've had decades like that."

Claire says, "I woke up thinking I'd be nice and cook Poppy some French toast. So I open the egg carton and poke my finger through one of those stuck-on leaky eggs. When I got through cleaning the egg off the refrigerator, the milk turned out to be sour. I figured: Well, I'll make her scrambled eggs with coriander, she likes that. I went out to the garden for coriander and all the tomatoes were lying on the ground. The awful part was that most of them looked fine from on top, you had to turn them over to see they were smashed. You know, first you think it's all right, and then it isn't all right."

"I almost never think it's all right," says Raymond. "That's how I take care of that."

"Know how I took care of it?" says Claire. "I went crying to Joey. Then I went upstairs and got out these star decals I'd been saving. I thought it would make me feel better. I'd been planning to paste them on the ceiling over the tub so I could take a shower with all the lights out and the stars glowing up above, and even in winter it would be like taking a shower outside." Suddenly Claire is embarrassed by this vision of herself naked in the warm steamy blackness under the faint stars. She wonders if Dottie is listening from the other room and is almost glad the next part is about finding the shampoo bottle.

"That's life," says Raymond. "Reach for the stars and wind up with a bottle of piss."

"That's what I thought," says Claire. "But listen." She tells him about calling the girls in, and when she says "like newborn giraffes," she really does feel awful, as if she's serving her daughter up so Raymond will see her as a complicated person with a daily life rich in similes and astonishing spiritual reverses. Now she understands why she hadn't mentioned the incident to Dottie or Joey. She was saving it for Raymond so it wouldn't be just a story she'd told before. But Raymond's already saying, "I know. Sometimes one second can turn the whole thing around.

"One winter," he says, "Miranda was around two, she was sick all the time. We were living in Roxbury, freezing to death. We decided it was all or nothing. We sold everything, got rid of the apartment, bought tickets to some dinky Caribbean island where somebody told us you could live on fish and mangoes and coconuts off the trees. I thought, I'll paint shells, sell them to the tourists. But when we got there, it wasn't mango season, the fish weren't running, and the capital city was one giant cinderblock motel. There was a housing shortage, a food shortage, an everything shortage.

"So we took a bus across the island, thinking we'd get off at the first tropical paradise, but no place seemed very friendly, and by then Miranda was running another fever. We wound up in the second-biggest city, which looked pretty much like a bad neighborhood in L.A. We were supposed to be glad that our hotel room had a balcony facing main street. Dottie put Miranda to bed, then crawled in and pulled the covers over her head and said she wasn't coming out except to fly back to Boston.

"At that moment, we heard a brass band, some drums. By the time I wrestled the balcony shutters open, a parade was coming by. It was the tail end of Carnival, I think. The whole island was there, painted and feathered and glittered to the teeth, marching formations of guys in ruffly Carmen Miranda shirts with marimbas, little girls done up like bumblebees with antennae bobbing on their heads. Fever or no fever, we lifted

Miranda up to see. And maybe it was what she'd needed all along. Because by the time the last marcher went by, her fever was gone.

"Miranda fell asleep, then Dottie. I went for a walk. On the corner, a guy was selling telescopes. Japanese-made, not like the one out there, but good. They must have been stolen off some boat—they were selling for practically nothing. So I bought one and went down to the beach. The beach was deserted. I stayed there I don't know how long. It was the first time I ever looked through a telescope. It was something."

For the second time that day, Claire's struck speechless. Only this time, what's astonishing is, she's in pain. She feels she's led her whole life wrong. What did she think she was doing? If only she could have been on that beach with Raymond looking through a telescope for the first time, or even at the hotel when he came back. Suddenly her own memories seem two-dimensional, like photographs, like worn-out duplicate base-ball cards she'd trade all at once for that one of Raymond's. She tells herself that if she'd married Raymond, she might be like Dottie now, confused and restless and wanting only to believe that somewhere there is a weed for her need. She remembers the end of the Hammett story: after Flitcraft's brush with death, he goes to Seattle and marries a woman exactly like the wife he left on the other side of that beam. There's no guarantee that another life will be better or even different from your own, and Claire knows that. But it doesn't help at all.

There's a silence. Claire can't look at Raymond. At last he says, "If I could paint what I saw through that telescope that night, do you think I'd ever paint another dancing vegetable in my whole fucking life?"

For all Raymond's intensity, it's kind of a funny question, and Claire laughs, mostly from relief that the moment is over. Then she notices that Dottie has come in. Dottie looks a little travel-worn, as if she might actually have crossed the steppes from Moscow to Paris. She seems happy to be back. As it turns out, she's been closer than that. Because what she says is, "Suppose I'd believed that old lady and dropped her off in the middle of Montpelier? What would have happened then?"

Claire wants to say something fast before Raymond starts inventing adventures for a crazy old lady alone in Montpelier. Just then, Joey reappears. Apparently, he's come back in and gone upstairs without their hearing; he's got the girls ready for bed, scrubbed and shiny, dressed in long white cotton nightgowns like slender Edwardian angels. Claire looks at the children and the two sets of parents and thinks a stranger walking in would have trouble telling: Which one paints dancing vegetables? Which one's lived before as a Napoleonic soldier? Which ones have mated for life? She thinks they are like constellations, or like that engraving on Evelyn's father's desk, or like sunflowers seen from below. Depending on how you look, they could be anything.

Then Raymond says, "It's almost midnight," and they all troop outside. On the way out, Raymond hangs back, and when Claire catches up with him, he leans down so his lips are grazing her ear and says, "I hope this doesn't turn out to be another Comet Kohoutek."

Outside, Claire loses sight of them, except for the girls,

whose white nightgowns glow in the dark like phosphorescent stars. She lies down on the grass. She's thinking about Kohoutek and about that first winter she and Joey lived together. How excited he was at the prospect of seeing a comet; and later, how disappointed! She remembers that the Museum of Natural History set up a dial-in Comet News Hotline which was supposed to announce new sightings and wound up just giving data about Kohoutek's history and origins. Still, Joey kept calling long distance and letting the message run through several times. Mostly he did it when Claire was out of the house, but not always. Now, as Claire tries not to blink, to stretch her field of vision wide enough for even the most peripheral shooting star, she keeps seeing how Joey looked in those days when she'd come home and stamp the snow off her boots and see him—his back to her, his ear to the phone, listening. And now, as always, it's just when she's thinking of something else that she spots it—that ribbon of light streaking by her so fast she can never be sure if she's really seen it or not.

E V E R Y O N E
Had a
L O B S T E R

[veryone had a lobster. This
was a serious problem. Roy, the SoHo contractor who'd served
as a kind of treasurer for the lobster dinner, took Valerie aside
and said he was sorry it wasn't pasta or bouillabaisse, something stretchable. Valerie should have telephoned in advance,
they would have bought a lobster for her. Valerie thought:
Shut up. Her friend Suzanne—Roy's girlfriend, in fact—had
specifically told her not to arrive till after dinner; she said

Valerie should start being discreet about having lived in the summer house for six weeks without having paid any rent.

The others, a lawyer, two therapists, a cameraman, a painter, a contractor, and so forth—were splitting the rent of this mini-Versailles with its enormous restaurant kitchen, its *Citizen Kane* fireplace, its French doors facing on Block Island Sound. But no one seemed to mind that Valerie didn't contribute. They found her entertaining. They were all around thirty and felt that they used to know more people like her. They said she was right out there, right on the edge, by which they meant she had no income and was a bit manic, lean, a fearless swimmer, she had a terrific tan. Besides, they only saw her on weekends. They worked weeks and came out Friday nights, everyone but Suzanne, who was on vacation from teaching high school and had sublet her place in the city. Weekdays, the house had felt empty, so Suzanne had tracked down Valerie at her parents'. Valerie came for a visit and stayed.

Valerie liked the house, the shore. And Suzanne was her oldest friend. But by August some things about her life here felt like a job, a receptionist's job, not the chilly receptionists of the rich, but of those borderline businesses that hire you to be constantly cheery and up. Once Valerie had had such a job, at a carpet wholesaler's. Her boyfriend then often had speed, and she would do just a little before going to work. She wouldn't take speed now—it was so hard to get and terrible on your teeth—but she'd found an African bark called kava-kava you could buy at the health food store and chew and get a noticeable buzz.

She needed it to stay up, especially after a day like this, a whole boiling summer Saturday driving the Long Island

Expressway after Suzanne suggested she clear out for the day, keep a low profile for once. Valerie had planned to go to the city; the museums would be air-conditioned and empty. But she didn't expect so much traffic in that direction, stalled, overheated cars, thirty miles of steam pouring out from under hoods, and her chewing kavakava, so that finally she pulled off the road and followed signs to a state park where she was the only white person on the beach.

At first this was a little disconcerting: she gave the groups of Puerto Rican guys a wide berth, but no one seemed even to notice her, or pay any attention. It was as if she wasn't just white, but transparent. The point was, everyone was busy with their own good times. She stayed there all day, and later stopped at a Chinese restaurant where she ordered a dish of day-glo orange sweet and sour pork she would have been embarrassed to eat in front of anyone she knew.

She was positive that the people at the summer house would be long finished with dinner, but she walked in to find the table elegantly set, each individual lobster leaking cloudy water onto its individual plate. At least twenty people were seated around the table and at least five or six of them called to Valerie—"Eat! There's steamers and corn!" Valerie said she'd eaten, relishing the memory of her sweet and sour pork. They would be horrified, or else mistake her pleasure in it for some interest in edible kitsch. They were all very serious about food, they planned elaborate menus, all shopped and cooked like some semi-pro catering crew. Suzanne and Valerie had always liked cooking and eating, but last week Suzanne told Valerie she was going to strangle the next person who said "radicchio."

As Valerie caught Suzanne's eye, it occurred to her that everyone was saying, "Eat! There's steamers and corn!" but no one was saying a word about lobster despite the humongous red ones sitting right there on their plates. Suzanne put her hands over her lobster, as if to protect it from Valerie, and Valerie knew she wasn't mad about her showing up too early.

Valerie was always telling Suzanne she was too paranoid about the other people in the house. Suzanne's problem was that she made the least money of anyone—though not little enough to seem brave, like Valerie—and that her boyfriend Roy made the most. Roy wore the three-piece suits, the ponytail and potbelly of a rich California dope lawyer. He was bisexual, he liked to talk about his leather-bar night life. Especially when someone new—someone innocent and shockable—was around, Roy could get pretty graphic. He said he didn't worry about AIDS, every six months he went to Rumania and had his blood changed. Sometimes he would say this right in front of Suzanne, and Valerie would thank God that she wasn't leading Suzanne's life.

Not that Valerie felt she was leading her own life, exactly. Lately she had the sense she was stuck in some pre-life, some in-between life, waiting for her serious life to start. For now, all that mattered was keeping interested. Lobsters were very low on her interest list, but she had to focus on them for a while before she could make herself look at Nasir, who was way at the top of the list. Nasir waited till she looked at him, then cracked the claw off his lobster, held it out to her, and at the same time motioned toward the seat next to his.

At that table, that art director's gourmet dream of perfect red lobsters on perfect sea-green glass plates, Nasir's ripping into that lobster seemed really kind of primitive and nasty. But Nasir could get away with it because he was so beautiful and graceful, and was basically a nice guy. Also, Valerie noticed, he held the lobster body so the juice dripped on the plate.

Everyone got quiet and waited to see what Valerie would do. For weeks she and Nasir had circled each other; it gave the atmosphere an erotic charge and was part of what people found entertaining. Valerie would have liked to sit next to Nasir. She was so drawn to him it scared her. One problem was Nasir's girlfriend, Iris, sitting across from him. But that wasn't it, exactly. No one liked Iris, and Nasir cheated on her constantly; last winter he and Suzanne were involved for about two weeks.

Nasir was Pakistani, British-educated, with a terrible and romantic history of loved ones disappeared into Zia's jails. Unlike everyone else in the house, all of whom were their professions, Nasir shot commercials for a living but was actually something else—a Marxist who dreamed of making political documentaries. So he too was more like the people these people used to know, and maybe that was part of the kinship Valerie felt with him. Also, they shared a similar manic edge. He was the only one she could have taken to the state park, the only one who would have seen what she saw in that Cantonese restaurant extravaganza of red and gold.

The last commercial Nasir shot was for a manufacturer of remote control lamps. Last weekend, Nasir brought twenty lamps out to the house and put them around the living room, and they all took turns standing in the center of the pitch black room making twenty lights dance on and off with the remote control wand. Nasir was always surprising them, turning out to know card tricks, to play stride piano and an amazing game of soccer. He had very large brown eyes, and the power of his attention was such that now, as Valerie laughed and shrugged off his lobster offer, she was so adrenalinized and trembly she had to sit right down next to Suzanne.

Suzanne said, "You chicken." She was all for Valerie having a romance with Nasir—partly, Valerie suspected, because then the responsibility for Valerie's continued presence would no longer be just Suzanne's. Last week, when they were alone in the house, Suzanne told Valerie that she and Nasir would be good together, they both had great bone structure. It was something a fifteen-year-old would say, but Valerie couldn't help asking, "Really?" or being embarrassed by how happy it made her.

Based on her own little fling with Nasir, Suzanne has warned Valerie not to expect too much, so Valerie could hardly tell her that what held her back, what kept her from even taking a lobster claw she might have liked, was that she expected the world, she had a sense that what happened with her and Nasir could be serious. She could imagine a life with Nasir, or anyway, time enough to find out who he was.

Dutifully, Suzanne asked if Valerie wanted a bite of her lobster, and Valerie said no, she didn't want to spoil her high, and showed Suzanne her little plastic bag of kavakava. Suzanne made a face. Up and down the table, they were talking about food. Roy was going on about lobsters, information he'd picked up from the man at the fish store, many incredibly boring facts about water temperature and seasons. Then Nasir said that when he first came to this country, he'd worked briefly at a restaurant with a fresh water tank in which there was one lobster no one would touch, a forty-eight-pounder named Captain Hank.

Someone asked Nasir where he'd been today, and he said, "I ran away with Valerie." Valerie was so shocked she laughed idiotically and said, "No, he didn't!" And where was Valerie? Valerie described the beach she'd been to as if she'd headed there on purpose, and when Roy asked how it was, she said, "Oh great, just like Carnival in Rio! You would have loved it, Roy!" Then she asked how *their* day at the beach had been, and after a funny silence, everyone said fine.

Valerie said, "What are you guys not telling me?" Suzanne whispered, "Hey, be quiet, okay?" But before anyone could answer, Valerie stood up—the kavakava was making her thirsty and unable to sit still. There was only wine and beer on the table; it would have been okay pharmacologically, but mixing alcohol and the root left a bad taste in her mouth. As she filled a glass at the kitchen sink, she heard someone behind her.

Nasir came close and said, "Wait till you see what's on today's tape. I'm gone a few hours and all hell breaks loose."

One custom of the house was that they videotaped the whole day—breakfast, grocery shopping, the beach—and watched it after dinner on TV. The only event left undocumented was dinner, which they were too busy eating to shoot. Mostly Nasir did the taping, the equipment was his, but he had shown everyone how to use it, and in his absence, Iris generally took over.

"Don't tell me—an orgy," said Valerie. Nasir just laughed, as did Valerie, thrilled by their apparent agreement that an orgy without the two of them seemed truly beneath contempt. "Then what?" she said. "A murder?"

"Believe me," said Nasir, "a murder would look healthy. Fun. Compared to what they've got taped, a murder would look like nursery school."

"Wow," said Valerie. But Nasir wouldn't say more. He said he hadn't seen it, only heard, and now it was hard for Valerie to insist, with ten people carrying in dirty lobster plates while ten more came in debating the best way to unmold crème caramel.

After dessert and the coffee, which took forever because the cappuccino machine could only make four cups at a time, they settled around the living room in front of the TV and turned off all the lights. Nearly everyone sat near the small screen, except for Valerie, who was chewing kavakava and pacing, and Nasir, standing and leaning against the back wall, his face lit and shadowed dramatically by the flickering TV.

The first shot was of people loading the van to go to the beach, and when the camera slipped and the picture swooped down, someone watching said, "Terrific, Iris."

The camera was riding shotgun. Gary, the lawyer, drove. When Valerie had first come to the house, Gary was clearly interested, but seemed like someone so used to women refusing him that she never even had to say no. Now he played to the video camera, giving his impression of a tour bus guide running down the sights. Gary shouldn't have tried, he was stiff at it, and faltered. Iris's camera caught every wrinkle of strain. Iris was a therapist, she used video in counseling, and somehow everyone she photographed looked as if they were toughing it out at some family crisis session. When Nasir did the taping, people looked more handsome and relaxed.

At the beach, Iris caught lots of unfortunate close-ups: squinty eyes, hairy backs, even some arm-skin flapping as shirts were pulled up over heads. Valerie thought: Trust Iris to show them the suddenly unmistakable signs of age. The camera made it obvious that Roy wouldn't take off his Hawaiian shirt, the audio blurred the drone of his voice as he sat on the sand holding court like some obese Polynesian king. Keeping its distance, the camera turned on a handful of people walking gingerly into the surf. Then Gary—not on the tape but in the room—said, "Oh, here's where I almost drowned."

"Here's *what?*" said Valerie, kneeling down at the back of the crowd around the TV.

"Almost drowned," Gary said, but just then the camera was occupied with a start-up soccer practice. Nasir had introduced the game to the house; they played often. Without him, the guys kicking the nerf ball around all looked a little adrift. Then a woman's voice—on the tape but off camera—said, "Hey, look out there!" and the lens turned toward the horizon where now in the water you could see a human form, moving oddly.

Another off-camera voice asked who that was, and someone else said, "I think it's Gary." A couple of seconds went by, then somebody asked, "You think he's in some kind of trouble?" Another pause, then somebody else said, "No." The camera turned back to the soccer players standing there lamely, like couples between dances, watching the ocean till someone said, "Are you sure he's all right?" Focus on Suzanne looking out at the water, then shrugging and saying, "I think he's okay," then going off to check something in the food hamper; the camera followed her the whole way, which took about a minute.

"Hey," said a voice on the audio track, "look at that!" The screen went black. Someone in the room said, "Jesus, Iris, this is where you blew it?" "Sand on the heads," Iris said. "I had to switch it on and off a few times."

When the image returned, the lens was scanning the water till it found that same form moving in place and two others speeding toward it. And now the camera zoomed in on two guys grabbing Gary and dragging him in toward the shore. This took a long time, too, finally everyone was wrapping towels around a gagging, shaking Gary.

Gary, in the room, said, "Thank God for the Coast Guard."

"You almost died," said Valerie. "Gary almost died, you guys."

"All right, Valerie," said Roy. "We can't all be world-class swimmers."

"You sons of bitches," Gary said. Then he laughed.

Valerie said, "I can't believe this."

Someone close beside her said, "You'd better believe it." It was Nasir. Valerie grabbed his shoulder and pulled herself toward him and began to whisper in his ear, but it wasn't sexual, really, it was like talking into a disembodied ear, the only one that would listen to her as she went on whispering, a hot, slightly sandy whisper. The kavakava had begun to burn her mouth. She asked what was wrong with these people, how could Gary sit there and joke with these assholes who had almost let him drown, who were too selfish and lazy to even find out if he had been drowning, and maybe for a little while, at dinner, knew they'd done something wrong, but seeing it on video had freed them, had let them pretend it was just something else on TV.

Nasir didn't answer. Instead he very gently placed his hand on the back of Valerie's neck. Valerie felt slightly queasy with lust, felt literally slightly sick. The warmth of his hand drew everything to the back of her neck, but everything was confused—sex, anger, exhaustion, fear, the kavakava which suddenly tasted awful. She said, "Christ. I need air."

She went out onto the lawn which sloped down to the Sound. It was a clear night and in the distance she could make out the lights of Block Island. After a while she heard people outside, near the door, getting the mountain of wood needed to make a fire in that cavernous fireplace.

When they'd gone in, and smoke was coming from the chimney, she went to the woodpile and got the smallest pieces and began to stack them near the far end of the lawn. She made many trips, adding on branches which had fallen during a rainstorm last week and still lay around on the grass. When she had enough for a sizable bonfire, she sneaked back into the house. Everyone was watching the fireplace, or reruns of SCTV. She ducked into the kitchen and got newspapers and a bottle of brandy.

The fire flared up so fast she jumped back. It went up in two stages, first it rose to two feet, then to about fifteen feet and stayed there, burning. Valerie stood with her back to the house, as near to the fire as she could. The fire didn't seem hot enough; she kept hugging herself and shivering. She imagined people up at the house, looking out the windows, laughing, maybe even applauding Valerie's latest crazy stunt. Then they would go back to the TV, or the bigger, nearer fire of their own.

Valerie really did feel crazed as she began to pace, slinking back and forth by the fire, like something out of *Cat People*. She gazed into the flames, putting herself in a kind of a trance which it took her some time to snap out of when Nasir came up beside her. "Great fire," he said.

"Thanks," said Valerie.

Then he said, "Give them a break, okay? They're scared too. Are you one hundred percent certain that you would have jumped in and saved him?"

Valerie was ninety-nine percent certain that she would at least have made sure someone did. But Nasir's words made her stop and think about the group in the house, about the terrible power of politeness, the desire that things remain civilized and well-mannered, the awful paralysis of the grateful guest. She looked back at the house and thought: No one lives there, no one has stakes there. They're all one another's guests.

It made her treasure Nasir even more, for quieting that part of her which was usually so harsh and quick to condemn. She thought: With Nasir, she would be a better person. She looked up into his face. They began to kiss, sweetly at first, then harder. After a while Nasir tipped his head back and as Valerie kissed his neck, he said, in a husky voice, "What about Suzanne?"

"What *about* Suzanne?" said Valerie.

"You two are friends, right?" he said. "Good friends. You can get her to come out here . . . the three of us . . ."

Valerie said, "No way."

Nasir laughed and hugged her. "All right," he said. "It

doesn't matter." He kissed her a couple more times. But really, it mattered a lot, it beamed like a laser straight to the part of her brain that governed desire. It cut that part right out. All Valerie could see was herself and Suzanne and Nasir, like some sleazy cameraman might see them, pale blond Suzanne, dark Valerie, Nasir darker still. It amazed her that what you'd hoped was the start of your life could turn out to be a scene in someone else's porno movie.

Nasir said, "Okay, later maybe," and straightened his clothes and walked back up to the house. Valerie just stood there. After a while she caught a whiff of smoke from the fire which reminded her of autumn, and she thought how often in fall she had driven along the edge of the forest, beside all the color, and imagined it would be even brighter inside, inside the woods and that beauty. So she would park and walk into the forest, but it was worse there, the light was wrong, you couldn't see far enough, it had been brighter from the road. Now she stared at the fire, at the changing shapes, and thought how the very worst moments of waiting for life to begin are better—much better—than knowing it already has.

CREATURE

COMFORTS

Rice taps his skinny, suntanned chest. He says, "Would I stiff my own brother?" On his face is the fixed, slightly glassy smile of a passenger in a convertible, going fast.

Nicky and Kate can't look at him. They can't even look at each other. They've been on the edge of a kind of hysteria since Rice's wife Pammy said, "That's some gigantic jade plant you've got there," and they both remembered how, when their twins were born, Pammy said essentially the same thing about the babies' ears. It's been eight years, the twins have grown into their ears, but other things have happened. Once, in an argument about nuclear power, Pammy said she was for anything that let her keep her creature comforts. Creature comforts! Rice and Pammy live in downtown Phoenix, in what used to be a motel cabin.

Once a year, around Christmas, they drive down to Tucson with gifts for the twins. Kate and Nicky had assumed this was one of those visits until Rice announced that he would be working in Tucson all January and wanted to live in the guest house in Kate and Nicky's backyard. Now he is trying to re-assure them that he can be trusted to pay his share of the electric bill.

Rice's question hangs in the air. Would he stiff Nicky? Probably. But that's only one of the reasons he shouldn't live here. Rice drinks too much, smokes too much dope; at least he's quit stealing cars. Twelve years of marriage to Pammy have pacified him; now it's just credit-card trouble, and, rarely, trashing his living room. Still, Rice is family, and they cannot refuse, cannot tell Nicky's younger brother he can't stay in the empty guest house. Also Nicky will be away that month—in L.A., where he goes periodically to work as a recording engineer. Kate would sooner have Rice here than no one. The Courtly Rapist with his knife and good manners is the current media star.

Everyone is trying so hard that Kate actually pretends disappointment when they learn they're not getting Pammy too. Pammy can't leave her office job in Phoenix, so Rice will commute home on weekends. Kate even feels compelled to thank Pammy on behalf of the jade plant. Then she says, "I don't know—it does better if you neglect it."

"That wouldn't work in my house," trills Pammy in her cartoon-mouse soprano. "I'm a kind of a witch about plants. I just look at them and they die."

Right at that moment the meat grinder falls down off the top shelf, narrowly missing Nicky. Nicky says, "Who did that?"

If Kate looks at Nicky she'll laugh. Though maybe Rice and Pammy wouldn't notice, they hardly flinched when the meat grinder hit the floor. There is a silence as everyone stares at the meat grinder. Finally Kate says, "Gee, I forgot we had that."

"I mean it," says Rice. "You think I'd beat my own brother on a bill?"

Kate feels a bit panicky. To no one in particular she says, "Know what I just remembered? Someone once told me that in India, the worst thing you can call someone is brother-in-law. It means you did it with his sister."

Pammy stares fixedly at the jade plant. Only when Nicky catches her eye does Kate realize what a strange thing she's just said. The reason she could say it at all was that no one here is likely to do anything with anybody's sister or brother-in-law. That Rice will be here alone with Kate doesn't register in that way. Rice isn't exactly someone you'd change your whole life to get close to.

Rice bursts out laughing, waving his arms; ashes fly from his cigarette. "Brother-in-law," he says. "That clinches it."

Nicky shows Rice what he needs to know about the guest

74

house. They carry out a frying pan, an electric heater, extra blankets. Then they arrange it that Rice won't move in until late the day Nicky leaves. Nicky tells Rice that his presence would drive him over the edge when he's getting ready to go.

There's a brief, uneasy silence. Then Rice says, "Hey, I can dig it," and punches Nicky's arm. The two couples exchange quick, stiff-armed hugs. From the cab of Rice's truck, Pammy calls, "You take good care of those kids!"

Nicky has been gone so much that Kate is almost used to it. Still, his leaving is hard. There is always that moment of wanting to call him back, to say: Let's sell the house, give in and move to L.A. All day, Kate's thoughts keep edging toward horrors she'll have to handle alone. The only thing that helps is cleaning the house. Housework can be so narcotic. Often she is surprised at her life, amazed that the kids and cooking and working in the garden could have turned out to be enough. But when Nicky is gone, she can no longer take pleasure in things themselves. It all feels as if she is showing someone: Look what I've done, at the hours I've passed, how much less time is left until he comes home.

Around when the children are due back from school, Kate is careful to be busy with something involving, like scrubbing the vegetable bins, so she won't notice if their bus is a few minutes late. Ben and Rachel know Nicky will be gone, but when they walk in and see Kate, their faces fall, like adults seeing a set dinner table and realizing that they are the only guests.

The sunset is spectacular, but it's one of those nights when all that blaze and color seems a little much. Kate realizes she is waiting for Rice, and is so glad to hear his truck in the alley that it takes her a while to get mad when he opens the alley gate and drives onto the back lawn. As he closes the gate behind him, she glares at him through the kitchen window, but he is too far away to see. He carries a cardboard box into the guest house, then comes out for an armload of books.

On the day he and Pammy came down, Rice said he was going to use his time in Tucson to do some heavy spiritual homework. Kate guesses that the books are part of this; she thinks of dreary Christian bookstores and the glossy bios of Indian gods Hare Krishnas sell at the airport.

Rice goes out to the truck one last time. Standing by the open cab door, he kneels and holds out his arms. And Pinky, Rice and Pammy's Siamese cat, jumps from the cab onto his shoulder. Pinky has been to Tucson before. Pammy won't leave the cat home; she worries it's anorexic. But why has she sent it with Rice? Pinky is old, incontinent, and noisy. Kate wants to run outside and fling Pinky back in the truck. Instead, she has one of those moments in which she's stricken with compassion for Pammy and Rice. When Rice knocks on Kate's door and asks if he can call Phoenix collect, she doesn't even mention Pinky. She says sure, he can use the phone, and how's the house? Rice says fine. Then he sniffs and says, "Mmmm . . . Mexican."

Kate thinks: Any normal person would invite Rice for dinner. But Rice is the one who's not normal. With him, it's only one step—one small step—from knocking politely on your door to coming in when you're not home and emptying your refrigerator.

Kate shrugs, and with a look of slight distaste says, "Oh, it's just something the kids will eat."

"That's okay," Rice says. "Pammy sent me down some stuff she fixed and froze to get me through the week. These really super egg rolls. She's really into egg rolls."

Egg rolls? Pammy is the microwave frozen-dinner queen. For as long as Kate can remember, Rice and Pammy have been on a beef and chemical diet. Pammy once told Kate about an article she read which said mankind needed a small steady dose of preservatives to carry on evolution. Most likely the egg rolls are part of the spiritual work. Well, really: Rice and Pammy are just the type for some major religious conversion. Kate is about to ask him what's in the egg rolls when he picks up the phone.

Kate goes into the living room to give Rice some privacy, but for once, the TV is off, the children are in their rooms, and though she makes an effort not to, she can't help overhearing. "How's Daddy's little sweetie?" Rice says. He listens and answers, "Fine, fine, me too." Then his voice drops and gets unintelligible, musical, cooing some private code of affection. Is it English? It's more like what Kate used to worry about—and listen for—when she'd hear stories of twins with sinister secret languages. For a moment it crosses her mind that maybe Pammy really *is* a witch, and this is their witchy talk. Then she thinks: Get hold of yourself. Pammy is much too straight.

When Rice hangs up, Kate stares at him. He says, "Don't

worry. I called the phone company last week. I'm getting my own line put in."

"Fine," says Kate. She busies herself at the stove. After a minute she says, "Did you check that with Nicky?"

"No," Rice answers. "Why?"

Kate calls, "Ben and Rachel! Dinner!"

Rice says, "I'll just stay and say hi to the kids. Then I'll be on my way."

Tonight the kids take even longer than usual to come. Sometimes Kate keeps yelling their names, but now she just stands there looking stupidly at Rice. At last the children slouch in. "Hey," Ben says to Rice. Rachel doesn't acknowledge him. Rice says, "See you guys," and leaves.

The kids sit at the table, hungry, barely patient. Kate gets them their enchiladas. Often, at mealtimes, Kate remembers how sometimes when they were babies, she caught herself feeding one the peaches that the other had just spit out.

"What's *he* doing here?" asks Rachel.

Ben says, "What planet are you on? That was all anyone talked about before Dad left. Dummy."

"Dummy?" says Rachel and twists the thin flesh on Ben's forearm. Ben pushes her away. The silverware jumps on the table. Kate just stands there. She would do anything to keep them from harming each other, but sometimes, when they are like this, she freezes as she used to when stray dogs would get in the yard and start dogfights with Buster. She would watch until Nicky reached into the snapping, churning mess, dragging Buster out and, miraculously, not getting bitten. Kate almost misses all that; lately Buster just sleeps.

Ben leans forward and yanks Rachel's hair. Rachel bursts into tears. Ben stands up from the table. "I think I'll go see what Rice is doing," he says.

"I'd rather you wouldn't." Kate's voice has an urgency so rare and authentic that even the children hear it.

"All right," says Ben. "But she'd better leave me alone."

"You kids are just hungry," Kate says.

Next morning, Kate points the man from the telephone company toward the guest house, then imagines Pinky streaking past him through the open door and vanishing forever into the alleyways of Tucson. Pammy will, of course, blame Kate. Kate runs after him, crying "Wait!" and muttering unintelligible half-sentences about the cat.

The telephone man is young, with longish hair, not the type to turn them in if Rice has left rolled joints and a mirror and razor blade in the middle of the living-room floor. He smiles as Kate says more than she needs to about her sister-in-law's overbred Siamese. Kate opens the door and steps cautiously into the cool dark interior of the house.

There is no problem locating Pinky, who is yowling at them from the round oak kitchen table where she sits, tall and cool as a fifties ceramic cat, perfectly still but for the yelling. "Shut up," the telephone man says, then glances at Kate to make sure it's all right. It's a moment of peculiar intimacy; then the phone man starts checking the walls for the jack.

"Funny house," he says. The white stucco walls are indented, inside and out, with the impressions of a giant clam shell.

"I love this house," says Kate. "When the kids get bigger, we're going to give them the other house and move out here." Kate has said this before, but suddenly it strikes her as impossible. What would she do here when Nicky's in L.A.?

"Oh yeah?" says the phone man. "You could rent this."

"We've talked about it," says Kate. In fact what they've said is: Let's rent it and live on the rent. Forget work, forget California, live on rice and tortillas and beans.

While the phone man works, Kate looks through a stack of paperbacks on the table. This seems to make Pinky yell louder, so Kate picks the cat up and puts her on the floor. The first book is *Diet and Spiritual Health*. The second is *Food for This World and the Next*. The third is, *Rational Fasting*. The fourth, *Cell Deprogramming*. The fifth, *Eat Less and Love More*. They are all about food and the spirit, not macrobiotic exactly, but filled with strange diet suggestions.

"Your brother-in-law go to school?" the phone man says.

"No," answers Kate, "he's a carpenter."

In front of the books, and closer to the table edge, is a diary, navy velvet and gold, with gilt edges and a small gold lock—unlocked. Kate runs her hand over the plush cover, then quickly turns away. When the phone man goes out to the truck, Kate opens the diary to the first page of writing. She'd thought the book might be Pammy's, but the narrow, tilted script is definitely Rice's:

The cat is getting used to our new dwelling place. Already it has found its spot, like Don Juan says. When it sits on the table, it looks very Egyptian, which is funny because the guy who read Pammy's past lives said she was once an Egyptian queen. *The cat and I take our little meals at the same time. I read aloud to it. I want the cat to be prepared.*

Kate wishes Nicky were here. How they would laugh at the thought of Rice reading spiritual bits to the cat. She'd settle for telling the phone man, but cannot admit she's been reading a book plainly marked, in gold script, My Diary. When he walks in, she puts it down.

That night, on the phone with Nicky, she says, "He wants the cat to be prepared for *what?*"

"College," Nicky says. "Kitty College."

"The priesthood," Kate says, then shivers. It occurs to her that she hardly knows Rice. Nicky and he are twelve years apart; Nicky hardly knows him either. "Nicky, this could be bad. Anything could happen with Rice. He could be into some egg roll satanic magic—candles and Siamese cat sacrifice."

"Please," says Nicky, "Relax. Hard as it is to believe, the guy and I share a DNA code."

Kate says, "Maybe Rice is a mutation." But that isn't what she wants to say. There's something else she means to tell him, but she can't remember it, though she waits so long for it to come back that Nicky says, "Hey, girl, this is long distance."

When Rice leaves for work the next morning, the sound of his truck wakes Kate. Day is just breaking, and in the little house, all the lights are still on. Well, it's Rice's electric bill. Isn't it? *Would* he stiff his own brother? What if a wire overheats and starts a fire? Kate is incapable of leaving the lights on all day. She might as well turn them off now, in the few minutes before she has to wake the kids for school.

Out in the yard, the smell of creosote is strong; the winter sun is pale, the paloverde and the century plant give off a silvery light.

In the little house, Pinky is pacing the living room, making little whip turns at the corners; it crosses Kate's mind that the lights may have been left on for Pinky. That Rice and Pammy would do such a thing fuels Kate with an outrage that rockets her across the room to Rice's diary. Yesterday's entry is still the only one. Kate is keenly—surprisingly—disappointed. She looks around the house. But there is nothing to see, Rice has nothing here except the books, some jeans and T-shirts, and a small microwave oven. Kate opens the refrigerator, where she finds a few dozen egg rolls, each wrapped in foil and stacked in rows that remind her of a brochure she saw once, an ad for cryogenics. Pinky is crying louder. Does the cat live on egg rolls too? Kate is relieved to see a tin of Kal Kan with its lid pushed halfway down.

One day passes, then another. Kate's only contact with Rice is the sound of his truck, twice a day. She feels restless, on edge. Friends call, but she doesn't go out. When she thinks of Rice's diary, she thinks: Some questions are better unanswered. She thinks: Curiosity killed the cat, and laughs a little hysterically and thinks: I've been alone too long. Somehow the weekend passes. Rice and the cat come back Monday night, and on Tuesday Kate waits till the kids have left for school, then walks across the backyard.

Today she has no excuses. The lights aren't on, Pinky is

still in her spot on the table, but the diary is gone. Kate is aware of the cat watching her as she looks around the house. Finally she finds the diary in the bedroom, beside the mattress on the floor. Kate hasn't been in this room for years. Neither she nor Nicky have reason to. One reason they bought the house was so Nicky could build his own sound studio here. But there is no work in Tucson, and the guest house has become a reproach, like something new and never worn, still hanging in the closet.

There's so little here—a mattress, a blanket, sheets, a small metal tensor lamp, the diary—and what there is is so minimal, so makeshift, less like a bed than a place where animals bed down, but spookier, like those caves one comes across sometimes in the canyons, fitted out with piles of rags and sterno stoves. But it's also like a kid's bed, those warm, rumpled fortresses of covers. Sitting on the edge of the bed, on the thin, washed-out sheets, Kate makes herself touch the wrinkled place where Rice must have slept. Then she picks up the diary, rereads the first entry, and goes on to the second:

Our cells are the prisoners of protein. We must open them to new knowledge. Protein is only a program. We must re-program our cells for cellulose. Even the words go together. We see and hear with our cells. Our cells hear the screams of the slaughterhouse

And that's all. Why does it scare her that Rice has left off the period after slaughterhouse? The rest is so meticulous. It's crazy stuff, but no crazier than the stories one hears about the million-dollar health spa out on Orange Grove Road, its specialty coffee enemas. Rice can live without meat a few weeks, he can survive on egg rolls. But if cellulose is the point, why not celery, and why was Rice in her kitchen sniffing after the children's cheese enchiladas?

On the phone, Nicky says, "Doesn't beer have protein?" And there is that shift she hears in his voice when he's been gone a few days; though he cares deeply, the house's small problems are no longer his.

"You're thinking of vitamin B," says Kate. "Anyway, Rice isn't drinking. Or taking drugs."

"Rice not drinking or doing drugs?" Nicky says. "Jesus. Hey. Watch out."

Some nights, especially when they have chicken or veal, Kate thinks of sending one of the kids to get Rice. She tells herself she isn't his mother, but still some part of her worries about Rice at work using power tools on a protein starvation dict. Motherhood has changed her, she's become everyone's mother, protective.

Once more Kate finds herself watching for Rice—but now it's for proof that she needn't feel guilty, that Rice isn't wasting away. She's oddly proud of every day that passes without her snooping in Rice's diary. She even learns to live with the lights in the little house left on; it's a kind of discipline, or surrender. Spiritual homework.

One afternoon Rice comes to the door and tells Kate his truck needs its ignition rewired. He asks if she'd mind if he fooled around with it in the backyard, after work. Kate minds very much. Rice specifically promised Nicky to make himself scarce. But Rice is always putting you in this position: his survival versus your convenience. At least auto repair seems like a sign that protein deprivation hasn't damaged Rice's brain.

Rice and his truck take over the yard. Kate suspects him of using more tools than he needs. How many wrenches and ratchet sets and buckets and rags could rewiring require? Rice carries them out and in again each day. He is under the truck hood from when he gets home until dark, and though it irks Kate, she thinks: Well, better this than reading diet advice to the cat. What's hardest is the recurring image of all those grimy tools in the guest house, seeping indelible black gunk into the white cement floor.

In fact the reality is pretty much as she imagined, tools everywhere, little piles of greasy rags. Even Pinky has to share the table with a heap of pliers. But the books have been pushed to one side, and when Kate finds the diary—again, beside the bed—she is gratified to discover no entries past that second one, about reprogramming cells. Encouraged, she does a spot-check on the fridge, where, still, there are only egg rolls, stacked like tin-foil mummies.

It has been a mild winter, but suddenly it turns clammy, cold rain every day. Rice stops working on his truck. Now when Kate spots him out the window, Rice wears a dungaree jacket, and hunches, pale and visibly chilled. Kate worries about the nights—the little house can get very cold. On the phone Nicky says, "Well, sure. That's why we brought out the heater."

All morning Kate pictures the radiant heater, cooking away, streaming heat into the sofa or a brown paper garbage bag till the guest house goes up in flames. In any case, the electric bill will set a new world record. Around noon she goes over to check.

In fact, the heater is off. The little house is really quite chilly and Pinky is yowling nonstop. Not two feet from the heater are some tools, heaped-up rags and a closed can of gasoline. Kate cannot believe it. Not even Rice is that dumb. She thinks about Pinky blown clear out the window like some charred, frazzled cartoon cat. Then she feels slightly sick.

The diary is back on the table. The several entries past what she's already seen are all variations on this:

The cat is too dependent on me for its existence. I must teach it the art of rational fasting. It is easier down here. Pammy couldn't do it. In that way I am further along on the path. The cat is nearly liberated from protein. What is the point of freedom if Pinky can't be with us?

Kate takes a hard look at Pinky, but can't see any change; Pinky was always bone-thin. In the refrigerator is an empty, crusted-over catfood can. Kate runs back to her house, opens a can of Buster's food, then comes back and dumps it in Pinky's dish. Pinky dives right in. But is this extraordinary hunger or normal behavior? Kate has only Pammy's word that Pinky's a finicky eater. Cats are supposed to lick things clean—trust Pinky to leave smears of food on the dish. Kate cannot bring herself to rinse it.

On the phone Nicky says, "It's *his* cat, what do *you* care?" There's a silence and then he says, "Joke."

"I'll feed the cat," says Kate. "I just want to make sure he moves that gas can and those rags."

"Then tell him," says Nicky, as if it were as simple as that.

Kate rehearses it in her head, aiming for a breezy tone: Oh, by the way, about that gas can . . . And breeziness might be an option if she'd started one conversation with him the whole time he's been here. But now, even though—or because—he's putting them at risk, she feels she's been inhuman, done the minimum and no more. Not only that, she's read his diary, sabotaged what precious little dignity Rice has. She cannot start right in scolding, lecturing Rice on his home safety habits, all that practiced breeziness turning instantly stony and tense. She waits a day and goes back; the heater and the gas can are just where they were.

Soon after Rice gets back from work, Kate sends Ben over to invite him to dinner. Ben comes back almost immediately and says Rice is on his way. Is it okay if he brings the cat? Kate says, "So long as the cat doesn't pee on the kitchen floor." Ben says, "You tell him that," and laughs. Rachel says, "God. *Would* it?"

As usual, Rice's face—friendly, bland, his eyes not quite meeting hers—shows nothing. Pinky is perched on his shoulder. In his jeans and denim jacket, with his ponytail and wispy beard, Rice looks like those kids you saw fifteen years ago at be-ins and still see sometimes at crafts fairs. Even back then, you knew to stay away from the ones with animals on their shoulders.

Kate says, "Should I set a place for the cat?" Anyone else

would laugh. Anyone who was secretly starving his pet might betray a slight twinge of guilt. But Rice says, simply, "No thanks. I fed her before we came over."

How long before? thinks Kate. Three weeks? But she makes herself smile at Rice and says, "It's all ready. Please. Have a seat." Pinky stations herself on the floor behind Rice's chair; Kate is about to say how Egyptian Pinky looks when she recalls reading something similar in Rice's diary. Then she starts to ask what piece of chicken Rice wants when she remembers that the children are at that stage—they'll fall off their chairs if someone says "breast" or "thigh." So she gives Rice the serving fork and tells him, "Help yourself."

Rice takes a drumstick, a large dab of mashed potatoes and a stalk of broccoli and arranges them neatly on his dish. Kate remembers the old Rice heaping his plate and scarfing down mountains of food. Rachel and Ben stare at Rice—they've never seen a grown-up invest so much energy in making sure nothing touches. Rice waits till everyone is served, then takes a bite of mashed potatoes and a tiny piece of chicken and chews this mouthful forever. The kids look at him, then at Kate, then back. Kate says, "Kids, you're not touching your food." Without taking their eyes off Rice, the children begin eating—dutifully, almost as slowly as he does. Kate asks him, "How's work?" Rice nods pleasantly and keeps chewing.

After a while Rice takes a fingerful of mashed potatoes and, leaning down, feeds it to Pinky. Rachel says, "Ugh. Gross."

"She likes it," says Rice.

"I'll bet she likes chicken better," says Ben. Rice seems on the point of saying something, and Kate thinks now she'll have to deal with the consequences of a lecture on reprogramming cats. But Rice's face turns quizzical; he tears off a piece of drumstick and hands it down to Pinky, who tilts her head and eats it with no more or less relish than she showed for the mashed potatoes.

"Pammy would kill me for this," says Rice.

Kate considers the pros and cons of asking, then can't help herself. "Why's that?"

"Oh, I don't know," Rice says. "She's just kind of careful about what Pinky eats."

Rice watches Pinky briefly, then goes back to slow-motion eating. Well, Kate thinks, it's nice to know that what people write in their diaries isn't always true. No one on a serious protein fast would be lured off his diet by plain baked chicken.

Long after the children finish and go to their rooms, Rice is still eating. It takes all Kate's forbearance not to get up and start clearing the table. She runs soothing thoughts through her mind: In a week Rice will be gone and Nicky will be here and her life will return to normal. So she's actually slightly startled when Rice says, "Thanks, that was great."

Kate says, "I'm glad you liked it," with something like genuine warmth. And then, because she's given him that, she tells him in a rush that she had to go out to the little house, Nicky thought he might have left something there, and she couldn't help noticing the gas can right by the heater, and it's all right, she knows it's nothing, but would Rice mind moving the can so she can stop thinking about it?

First Rice says, "Listen, that gas can is *closed.*" Then he catches himself and says, "Yeah, sure, I can move it. No problem. Thanks for dinner." And he's gone.

By and large, Kate's pleased by how the evening went. She's

pretty sure Rice will move the gas can away from the heater. And she no longer has to feel guilty for not having fed her brother-in-law the whole time he was here. True, it was hard being patient, watching him chew. Later the children will ask about it, and she'll tell them he likes his food chewed well. That they are still young enough to accept answers like that encourages her and makes her think: There's time. When Nicky gets home they'll figure out how to never spend another month like this.

She stacks the dishes in the sink, then paints them with wavy lines of turquoise soap. She squeezes out as much soap as she needs and then goes on squeezing. She wishes she'd known as a child that grown-ups could do things like this and no one can tell them to stop. She fills the sink with warm water and, as her hands slide in, the pleasure is so intense she thinks: Do enough spiritual homework and every minute could be like this.

Outside the window, the moon is bright and almost full. The night is so clear Kate can see the moon's craters. The moon hangs in the sky like a giant iced cookie someone has chewed on and put back. And that's when she sees Rice. She says, "Jesus Christ," and her voice is a kind of a moan. She grabs the Mexican blanket off the couch and runs out. If she is very quiet, the children won't look out the window and see their uncle on fire, burning, stumbling out into the yard. But even if they don't see this, they will see something. Whatever happens after this, nothing will be the same.

The fire—a body on fire—looks as it does in newsreels and movies, only more orange, brighter, and much slower. Kate is running towards Rice as fast as she can, the yard isn't very large, but still it seems slow, there is so much time, time to think, to think and remember the most unrelated things: a quiz-show jingle, Nicky's phone number in L.A., exactly how her children sound when they're cheating and denying it, their voices strained and cracked, insistent, shrill, screaming that everything's fair.

T O M A T O E S

Vincent's father is dying, but Laurel, the physical therapist, comes for an hour every afternoon and acts as if something can still be done.

"Feel up to a walk?" she says. When Vincent's father nods, she wrestles him off the bed and, hugging him from behind, half stumbles, half waltzes him around the room. "That's great, Mr. DiStefano," she says. "Push against the headboard. Count. One . . . two . . . three. That's terrific."

Vincent can't look. Unfocusing his eyes, he concentrates on wondering how Laurel—who, though plump and sturdy, is fairly small—can bear his father's weight. Not looking reminds Vincent of watching scary movies as a kid—even when he hid his face, he always saw *something*. Today what he sees is the wet circle where Laurel's white uniform sticks like a tight, shiny skin to her back.

It's August, but Vincent's father is always chilly. Another thing Vincent can't look at is the air conditioner his parents brought with them from New Rochelle when they retired and moved here to the country to be near him. Vincent had thought: They won't need *that* upstate. But as it turned out, they did. Even on cool country nights, their bedroom was freezing, and they'd lie on the king-size bed, watching TV, slightly lizard-like and slow. Vincent's father used to talk about his boyhood: hot nights on Elizabeth Street, his whole family on the fire escape, wrapped in wet sheets, like mummies. He never got over his pleasure in being able to make his nights so cold. Now all that has changed. Laurel and Vincent's father are also slow, but differently, not lizards but dancing bears as they stagger in the heat.

Vincent can't remember ever seeing his father dance. He does recall his walk—the dignified, slightly stiff walk of a man who feared he was clumsy and from time to time would trip; but when he thought no one was watching, he moved with astonishing grace. What astonishes Vincent now is that any of them can stand *this*. At least when Laurel's here, his father seems—literally—in good hands. For that hour, Vincent feels somehow lighter, as does his mother, who uses Laurel's visit to sneak off to the kitchen and cook.

Vincent follows her, and sitting on a step stool, just watches. There is nothing to say. Until a few weeks ago, Vincent could distract her with stories about his kids. Now Rose has lost interest in the grandchildren. Vincent can't blame her, but is troubled that Rose should act so much warmer toward Laurel, who's been coming only six months. When Laurel bounces in, Rose grabs her shoulders and holds her. With Vincent, Rose kisses the air and says, "Go see Dad." Yet this, too, has come to seem right. Laurel touches Vincent's father in ways Vincent can't. It would never occur to him to kneel behind his father and prop him against his thighs and tell him to reach for the bedrails. Though Vincent is in pretty good physical shape, he'd be scared to.

Last week, in the bookstore of the college where Vincent teaches, he heard a woman ask for a book called *The Healing Touch*. Now Vincent wonders if that's what Laurel has. For by the time Laurel has got him back in bed, Vincent's father has perked up some; his face is flushed with blood.

"All right, now, you be good," Laurel says. "See you tomorrow, Mr. DiStefano." Vincent's father smiles and waves. While Rose walks Laurel to the door, he motions Vincent close to his bedside and whispers, "That Laurel is some hot tomato."

Vincent would like to see this as a sign of his father being more "like himself," except that he was never like that. For most of his life, he was a high-school principal with formal, old-country good manners, a Louis whom no one ever called Lou. When Laurel calls him "Mr. DiStefano," she could be one of his New Rochelle High kids, come to him for a talking-to—and whom he would *never* have called a tomato. But in some more basic way, calling Laurel anything *is* more like him. At least it shows some notice of, some interest in, some hanging on to this world. Most of the time he just drifts.

So Vincent times his own daily visits to coincide with Laurel's. Right after she leaves is when his father is most likely to ask about the kids or Vincent's wife, Marianne. Vincent used to bring grandchildren stories and conversation about the new oil burner or minor car trouble—news, such as it was. It depresses him that his father is no longer interested. Now, though it's no longer true, Vincent says what he's been saying all summer: "Marianne's got a great garden this year."

"Kids keep her busy?" says Vincent's father, and Vincent, as always, says, "Yup."

What news could he give him? Marianne and the kids have taken up fishing; at least twice a week they paddle a friend's boat out onto the reservoir and sit there, casting. As far as Vincent knows, they haven't caught anything. Vincent has never gone with them, though they always ask. He tells Marianne it's hard for him to sit still, and she says she understands. But does she? *She* can sit still, and so can the children, who usually can't be anywhere without fighting. They must not feel the pressure Vincent does: how little time is left. Marianne loves Vincent's father; she cries when they talk about him. But the fact is, Marianne's own father is a hale Lee Marvin type with a twenty-six-year-old wife. Though Marianne and the kids wear hats and long sleeves, they are all deeply tanned—much, much darker than Vincent.

Vincent can't tell his father this. His father would hate knowing that, however unintentionally, he'd come between man and wife. Two things he always took seriously: marriage and work. So seriously that even now when, surprisingly, he asks, "How long till school starts?" Vincent can't groan or roll his eyes or make any of the signs he'd make to another teacher or, he thinks, to any normal high-school principal in the world.

"Three weeks," Vincent says.

Vincent teaches French literature. His specialty is Flaubert, whom he teaches alternate years and will be teaching this fall. Right now he dreads it. Teaching *Madame Bovary*, he used to feel the thrill he imagined a world-class headwaiter might feel smoothly deboning a very complicated poached fish. Now he wonders how anyone could be thrilled by that. Lately he's been acutely aware of the skeleton, and of his father's bones softening. Sometimes the word "bone" crops up in his conversation, inappropriately. A while ago he told Marianne that her dusty, neglected garden would pep up if it just had a bone of rain. Bone of rain?

What's more, Flaubert makes Vincent feel doubly pathetic for having become, as he's finally admitted to himself, infatuated with Laurel. He feels like dopey Emma, pining for dull Leon. He wishes—has been wishing all summer—that he had studied Russian instead so he could be teaching Tolstoy, with his grand passions and grand punishments, or better yet, Chekhov, whose vision was broad enough to see that the slickest little flirtation could at any moment and without warning turn into something mysterious and profound.

Lately, doing the small, back-to-school chores—caulking windows, getting the car inspected—Vincent has been thinking about Laurel. He knows that she lives alone, in an apartment in Remsenville, and that her family is from Troy.

But that's all. They've hardly spoken, though he's thanked her a hundred times for what she's doing for his father. Laurel always says, "Oh, God, don't thank me. It's nothing." Then she smiles at him, and Vincent is aware of her tight little body, packed into her white suit. A tomato, he thinks. That's exactly what Laurel is.

One form Vincent's obsession takes is curiosity: How does his mother feel when Laurel crawls all over her husband of forty years? From what Vincent can gather, she's just grateful. What's between the three of them now transcends sex and jealousy—it's just tending to the body. Whenever Vincent eavesdrops on Laurel and Rose, they're exchanging recipes. Laurel is a serious cook; she talks of making crème brûlée, and Vincent thinks: Who for? But mostly those conversations give him the same sad feeling he gets when he finds himself eye-to-eye with Rose's spice shelf, with the pint jars of dried home-grown basil and oregano, unopened for months.

Laurel and Vincent's mother and father form a kind of triangle so pure that it makes him feel doubly guilty for having sexual fantasies about Laurel. He can imagine digging his fingers in her tight blond sheepdog perm, but not how they got to that point. He can't picture going to her apartment or to some motel, can't even see suggesting it.

So he tells himself it's not sex he wants. Lately, sex with Marianne has been complicated enough. One week passion is the only thing that matters. Some weeks he couldn't care less. No wonder Marianne wants to be out on that boat, with a whole reservoir between them. Vincent has never cheated on his wife, and though he knows that crises—like pregnancy, or death—drive people to break their own rules, they seem to him like strange times to start. Nothing, these days, is casual.

What he tells himself is, he'd be satisfied to just be alone with Laurel. Often he has conversations with her in his head. He asks why she became a physical therapist—that's one thing he wants to know. He also wonders if she has a boyfriend, and though there's no way he'd ever ask, he wants to know if the way Laurel moves with her boyfriend is anything—anything at all—like the way she touches his father. He would like to go somewhere, anywhere with Laurel—for a ride in the country or just a cup of coffee at some roadside greasy spoon.

Vincent hears Rose call, "See you tomorrow!" Looking out his father's window, he watches Laurel slide into her little blue Camaro. Before she leaves there is always a moment when he wants to go out and stop her. It's a little like the panic he feels sometimes when Marianne and the kids are leaving to go to the grocery.

Vincent so wants Laurel to stay that he feels slightly funny when Laurel buckles her seat belt, turns the key, and then frowns and turns it again. Nothing happens, and Vincent feels responsible, as if the magnetic pull of his longing could have actually shorted the wires in Laurel's car. He runs out into the driveway as if that will break the spell.

Vincent motions for Laurel to slide over. He gets in next to her, behind the wheel. He turns the key: there's a click. The car sounds completely dead. Vincent is very conscious of how close Laurel is. The front seat is so hot and small and intimate, they could practically be in bed. He closes his eyes, listening for that merciful one-second engine-splutter that sometimes lets you in. Laurel says, "I knew something was up. I drove all the way here with the battery light on."

"It's the alternator," says Vincent. The reason he can say this so confidently is that the same thing happened to his car earlier in the summer. Now he's almost glad that it did, and he feels that the two hundred dollars it cost was well spent. He asks if she has a mechanic.

"Sort of," Laurel says. "This one guy in Remsenville saved me when another guy in Troy was trying to rip me off for a whole new brake job when all I needed was the drums ground down and some shoes. You know the really awful part? The Troy guy had been my folks' mechanic for twenty years."

"That's terrible," says Vincent, but he's pleased by this image of Laurel—smart and plucky and sensible enough to go get a second opinion on her brakes. The fact that they're sitting here like buddies talking cars, talking brake shoes and alternators, encourages him.

"Remsenville isn't far," he says. "I'll drive you there, and maybe the guy can drive you back out here with a new alternator and some tools—put it together. It's really no big deal." Vincent is thinking, dispiritedly, that there's really no sense to this—it's easier to *call* the mechanic—when Laurel says, "I couldn't. I've got to be at a client's at four. This lady's only fifty, she's got Lou Gehrig's disease, and her second husband just left her. I've got to be there."

That Vincent's never considered who else Laurel might work for makes him feel small and self-involved and is partly why he says, "In that case I'll drive you *there* and wait till you're done and then drive you to the mechanic's."

Laurel twists toward him. Her left knee up on the seat, her

arm on the seat back, the curve of her breast against the upholstery—it's all one more thing that Vincent is trying not to see. "Oh, no," she says. "I *really* couldn't do that."

"Sure you could," Vincent says. "It's nothing for me— there's no place I have to be. I'd feel better . . . doing something. I mean . . . what you're doing for my father, I mean, I want to."

"Are you sure?" Laurel says. "You can still take it back." Smiling, she opens her mouth, turns her head to one side; light winks off a silver filling.

Vincent goes into the house. "Laurel's car won't start," he announces. "I'm running her over to her next appointment and from there to the garage." Vincent's father just smiles. At first Rose looks pleased that Vincent's doing something nice for Laurel, then satisfied, as if Laurel were some girl she'd been trying to fix Vincent up with, then worried, as if Laurel were a daughter Vincent was taking on a date. "What time will you be back?" she says. "What should I tell Marianne?"

"Jesus Christ," says Vincent, "just tell her what I'm doing." Then he says, "Sorry, Mom."

"That's all right," says Rose, and turns away from him. Vincent rarely sees Rose cry, but now there are tears in her voice as she says, "I know, I know. We've all got to blow off steam."

Vincent steers Laurel to his car. With baby Owen's car seat in the back, Beth's crayons and coloring books, and fast food garbage matted on the back floor, his car, he decides, is a half-ton wedding ring. Vincent remembers hearing about a sex murderer being sought in L.A. The witnesses are all prostitutes whose friends vanished forever after talking to some john with a kid's car seat in the back of his car. They disagree about what the guy looked like, but they all noticed that.

"How many kids do you have?" Laurel asks.

"Two," Vincent says.

"That's great," Laurel says. "I want to have kids. But I'm only twenty-five now. I figure I've still got time. Right?" She settles in, buckles up, then leans forward and runs one finger over the dashboard. "What kind of car is this?" she asks.

"Rabbit diesel," says Vincent.

"I've seen that ad," Laurel says. "Where Wilt Chamberlain gets out of the car?" Laurel sounds dubious, and Vincent can see why. Today the car feels small, mashing Vincent and Laurel together. The dark red interior fits them, close and hot as a blanket.

"Where to?" Vincent says.

Laurel laughs. "East Lexington," she says.

Vincent looks at her. East Lexington is twenty-five miles away. For a second he's annoyed, then excited, then happy.

"Are you sure that's all right? I can call a cab from Catskill." Laurel flutters her hands.

"I'm sure," Vincent says. "It's nothing."

It's a bright August afternoon, hot in the sun, but not humid. Driving through a shady patch, Vincent looks out at the cornfields; the edges of things are beginning to sharpen and turn crisp, like in the fall. The sky is a children's-book blue. Today—miraculously—they go five miles on Route 34 without seeing another car, and no trucks come barreling up behind them while Vincent's car strains toward the speed limit. "Hey," Laurel says. "Private road."

Neither talks for a while. No need to rush anything. Vincent slips a tape into the tape deck, and, as if on cue, the Talking Heads sing, "I've got plenty of time."

"Nice music," says Laurel.

Listening, they ride till they're just past Gilford Lake. Then Laurel leans forward again and turns the tape all the way down. Vincent likes the way she just went ahead and did that. Laurel points out the window at the former Arrowhead Lodge, now L'Auberge Colette, a French country inn opened last spring by two guys from Brooklyn Heights. Vincent has heard it's pretty good; some of the faculty go there.

"Have you ever eaten there?" Laurel says, and when Vincent says no, she says, "That's weird."

"Why?" says Vincent.

"You teach French," says Laurel.

Vincent waves one hand vaguely. "The kids . . ."

"You should get a babysitter," says Laurel.

"What about you?" Vincent says. "Ever babysit?"

Laurel giggles. "I'm not kidding," she says. "You should."

"You're right," says Vincent. They used to have a neighbor kid they thought was okay. One night they came home to find him showing the kids how to put lighter fluid all over his hand and set it on fire. But babysitter problems aren't what Vincent wants to talk about. Suddenly he feels that pressure again: time's running out. They're a third of the way to East Lexington. Soon he'll be dropping her at the garage and nothing will have happened but this.

"You can start off with this great grilled seafood sausage," Laurel says. "In a light tomato sauce with dill. And those crusty long baguettes to dip in the sauce—they bake them in this giant stone oven. Plus all kinds of terrines and pâtés with those little cornichons, I could eat a whole plate of them. The chef does great things with game. Venison with a kind of spicy Thai sauce. Stuff like that. Plus, you can get plain grilled fish, veal cutlets in this almond-lemon sauce. And for dessert—"

"Don't tell me," says Vincent. "Crème brûlée."

Laurel glances at him. "You don't have to eat there," she says, shifting slightly away in her seat. "I don't care."

"No," Vincent says. "It sounds great. Who do you go there with?"

"My cousin and her husband, mostly. They're into good food." Laurel moves closer again—all this is in fractions of inches. "Gee," she says. "Thanks, really, for the ride."

"It's nothing," says Vincent. That's right, he thinks. It is. Nothing. And what did he think it would be? What did he think would happen between him and some twenty-five-year-old physical therapist on the road between his dying father and a two-time loser with Lou Gehrig's disease?

Out of nowhere, there's a line of red brake lights ahead of him. Everyone's rubbernecking: a old man's car's broken down. For a while, after his father got sick, Vincent was always amazed to see old people walking around, or driving. This one's in trouble. Steam's billowing from under his hood. A cop's there, helping.

"Ruined *his* whole day," Vincent says.

"Car trouble all around," says Laurel. "Maybe it's in the stars." Laurel turns back for one last look at the steaming car, then says, "When I was a kid I thought I saw a vision in my neighbor's backyard. First I thought it was a ghost. Then I thought it was the Virgin Mary. But when I got really close it turned out to be steam from the neighbor's dryer."

Well, Vincent thinks, that explains everything. Religious. He's aware that some part of him wants to believe that Laurel is religious, that she'd have to be. In some way, Vincent decides, it's not her body he wants, but her spirit. He wants to believe that people like Laurel exist—simple, selfless, purely good.

"Are you Catholic?" he says. For a moment Vincent almost wishes he were; his parents stopped going to mass before he was born.

"Till I was seven," Laurel said. "Then I quit."

"Why'd you stop?" Vincent asks.

"I don't know. It was winter. It was cold in the church. I missed so much I just didn't go back."

Vincent thinks: If they've talked about God, they can certainly talk about work. "Listen," he says. "How does somebody become a physical therapist, anyhow?"

"SUNY," says Laurel. "I've only had my license three years."

"But *why?*" Vincent says.

"I just like to use my body, I guess," Laurel says. "Keep in shape. And I like to help folks."

Vincent can't let himself take this seriously. He doesn't even want to consider the possibility that this girl who has obsessed him, whom he's seen as a kind of saint with the healing touch, is in fact just a glorified aerobics nut. Besides, he's positive there's more to it. Certainly there are other ways to use your body and help folks besides lavishing such tenderness and encouragement on so much dying flesh.

"I guess that's not all," Laurel says a moment later. "I mean, for one thing, I was never squeamish about certain stuff that might bother other people. Even when I was little. Maybe I was born that way. Like here's something that happened." She waits a moment, then says:

"When I was ten we lived in a basement apartment in Troy. My window was right on the street. First it was a good neighborhood, then it wasn't so good, and one morning I woke up to find this bum in bed with me. It was summer and he must have crawled down through the open window. His face was stubbly, and at first I thought it was my dad—he always kissed me goodbye when he went to work. But then I smelled alcohol on his breath, and my dad didn't drink. The bum wasn't doing anything, just sleeping, but anyway I called my parents, and when they came in my dad went crazy, beating on the guy, pushing him out through the lobby and back onto the street. My mother would burst into tears whenever she told the neighbors. My brother had bad dreams for months. But not me. It didn't bother me, I don't know. Even then, I figured: Hey, he's a person, too."

Vincent loves Laurel's story, loves it so much he wants to make her repeat it. Maybe if she told it again, he'd know what it reminds him of. Then he figures it out on his own. It's "The Legend of Saint Julian Hospitaler," the story that, Vincent thinks now, was the most loving and beautiful thing Flaubert ever wrote. Julian, the hunter who has progressed from slaughtering the innocent beasts of the forest to accidentally murdering his own parents, is forgiven—and forgives himself—when he hugs a leprous beggar in his arms all night. Suddenly Vincent feels grateful for his work, for knowing that story and being able to make this connection. He feels that he has been allowed to see some pattern in things and feel comforted, feel that some things endure beyond individual lives. He remembers how when Marianne was pregnant with Beth, and he'd get scared, he'd look at strangers in the street and, for comfort, think: Everyone was born. Now he thinks: Everyone's parents die.

He so wants this feeling to continue that he tries to picture the Troy apartment, Laurel at ten. His daughter will be ten in three years, but dark, intense Beth is nothing like Laurel, and anyway, Vincent can never imagine his own children older. So he thinks of himself at ten, in his own room, his own house, the stucco New Rochelle Tudor they moved into when he was six. He sees his room, all those leaded glass windows, his toy trains—and instantly he realizes his mistake. The memory of that room is so sharply, so unexpectedly painful, it knocks the wind right out of him. For that was his father's house, where Vincent lived as a child. He will never live in that house again, and his father will soon be dead. Vincent sees that this fact stretches backward and forward in time, changing everything, so that even the happiest memories are dangerous and will hurt. What difference does it make if two stories match, if a French saint and some little girl in Troy wake up in the arms of a bum? His father is dying, and that's all there is.

"Are both your parents alive?" he asks. The way it comes out is almost accusing, which is almost how Vincent means it.

Laurel looks at him strangely. "Yes," she says. Then she says, "I'm sorry about your dad."

Vincent doesn't answer. He's afraid he'll start weeping in

front of Laurel. What makes it worse is that he can't even speed up to distract himself. He's stuck in a no passing zone behind some old lady doing forty. He leans forward, resting his breastbone against the wheel. Laurel leans forward too. He wonders if she's unconsciously mimicking him, then realizes she's pointing up through the windshield.

Looking up, Vincent sees a gigantic bird approaching them, flying slowly in from the west. At first he thinks it's a heron, but it's gliding. More like a hawk, except that it's too big for a hawk. Could it possibly be an eagle? Whatever it is, it's flying oddly, and as it gets closer, Vincent sees why. It's got a huge fish in its claws. The fish is still struggling, and the bird's trying not to drop it.

"I think it's an osprey," says Laurel. "Look at that!"

Still hanging on to the fish, the bird swoops down toward a telephone pole, clearly intending to land. But just as Vincent and Laurel pass, the fish drops out of its claws and falls to the ground. Vincent watches in his rear-view mirror as the bird hovers, checks out the wires, the nearby road, decides it's not worth it, and takes off. Vincent notices that the telephone pole is, as luck would have it, newer and slightly lighter than the rest.

Vincent and Laurel drive another quarter mile, till Vincent finds a safe place to make a U-turn. Then he circles around and heads back. He spots the light-colored telephone pole and pulls off the road. He gets out and walks through the grass.

The fish, still moving, is easy to find. Vincent picks it up. It's slippery and hard to hold, enormous and heavy and perfectly silver, shiny as a new dime. The sun hits it straight on. Its eye is open and bright.

He thinks about bringing it home. At first he is worried that Marianne and the kids won't believe him, or, if they do, will take it wrong: all their fishing brings in nothing, and all he has to do is drive down the road. He'll also have to explain what he was doing here with Laurel. Then he thinks: Marianne and the kids aren't like that. They'll believe him and love his story, they'll exclaim over the fish, his luck in finding it, his sharp eye, his reflexes, his common sense. His giving Laurel a ride will seem like what it is: a decent thing to do, regardless of why he offered.

Laurel is talking as she gets out of the car and walks toward him. "It's a freshwater bass," she's saying. "From the reservoir, probably. You can do anything with that. You could bake it in foil with plenty of fresh parsley and garlic and olive oil and green pepper and lots of sliced fresh tomatoes . . ."

Vincent can't speak. He holds the fish toward Laurel. He doesn't know if he is offering it or just showing it. He will do anything she says.

EVERYTHING
Is

About

ANIMALS

Her lover is a biologist, a specialist in animal relocation. When the ecologically conscious want to build in a wildlife area, he is called in to move the animal populations and accustom them to their new home.

It took her some time to believe that such a job really existed. Or rather, she believed him until the first time he went away on an assignment; then she worried that he had made it all up to escape her. It seemed inconceivable that men who constructed new factories and extended the edges of cities should spend so much money on nature. She could understand why the developers of a new ski resort might worry about displaced resentful bears, but why would a lumber company feel so solicitous about elk?

For comfort, she thought: How could anyone make all that up? Besides, the details of his life added up. He knew every animal language, every bird call, the moony lowing of bison, the high-pitched, complex rattling of hyenas. She loved hearing, but not watching, this; she was embarrassed by the comical ways he had to screw up his face to make these sounds. But often, at night, she'd ask him to do mourning doves or owls, and though it was already dark, she'd close her eyes and imagine her bedroom was a forest. Also she loves making love with him; she feels that watching animals mate has taught him something about men and women—nothing specific, really, but something she has no language for and so cannot describe.

What finally convinced her was nothing he did or said, nor the stories he told, nor the nature photos he showed her, but the charity ball he took her to, at which one hundred beautiful rich women signed pledges to never wear fur coats again. These women all knew him and spoke to him in hushed reverential tones; he smiled and lowered his handsome head toward their mouths. Then she realized that it wasn't the city planners or the corporate heads who were behind this, but the wives of the city planners and corporate heads. And now his stories made sense, made even more sense when he told her: these women would do things for animals, work and care for animals in ways they would never work or care for their fellow men. He is often hired to make sure animals get enough to eat in countries where people are starving.

She has learned to rely on him to make sense of the world. When they watch TV news, he tells her which criminals are innocent, which are guilty, and though his perceptions don't always match hers, she accepts his because she knows he reads deeper signs: lip curls, teeth baring, postures, blinks. She moves to the country, learns to live in the country—for the beauty and quiet, she says, but really to be more like the creatures he so admires. When he is with her, she thinks that this is the right way to live; at other times, she is more aware of the long commute to work.

She too is a scientist—a lab assistant, really. Her boss is a Korean biochemist who believes in the chemical nature of mental illness and gets grants to do elaborate analyses of the blood, sweat, and urine of schizophrenics. The other technicians are friendly, talkative women, mostly from exotic lands; at Friday lunch they have spectacular international potlucks. Ordinarily she likes her job, but when her lover is away, she makes frequent mistakes; the experiments require precise timing, and his absence distorts her sense of time. She has to concentrate on the clock, which only reminds her of how long until he comes home. Not that she knows. There is never any telling how long a herd of caribou, say, might take to accept their new grazing lands. She can't help being impatient and ashamed of her impatience, thinking of the animals, thinking: Hurry up and eat.

Also, there is this: to get to her lab, she has to walk down a long corridor past the animal research stations. The smell and the noise—the howls, the perpetual barking behind closed doors—are unspeakable. Usually she can steel herself and go deaf. But when he is gone she feels unworthy of him for not rushing in and throwing open the cages and letting the dogs and cats and rabbits run wild. She fears that her not doing this will undo all the points she imagines herself earning for having put in a garden.

Being with him has made her conscious of resources, of taking advantage. Partly for this, and partly to convince herself there were reasons to move to the country, she has planted a garden. Last year they did this together, but gardening alone is a bore. Now, just to make sure the sun and the smell of the earth don't trick her into happiness, she takes her ghetto blaster out for company and to drown out the sound of the breeze. She plays it loud, glad she lives in a place where there's no one around to hear. People used to talk about rock music killing plants, but her tomatoes do fine; they have grown two feet tall when the deer come in and eat everything. By August the deer are so tame you can yell at them and they will just stand there looking.

For two months she has been waiting for him to come back from Puerto Rico, where a new factory is displacing a colony of monkeys. The factory will make compact discs. Right from the start, this job irritated him. He said: CDs will never catch on. Leave the monkeys alone; in two years they can have the factory. She pictured monkeys perched on jungle ruins, sailing leftover CDs through the air like frisbees, like silver and rainbow UFOs catching the tropical light. But the company doesn't see it this way, and now the charity is paying him to move the monkeys deeper into the jungle's shrinking heart.

She has not heard from him since he got there. Mostly his

jobs are like this—miles from a telephone, mail that takes three weeks to come. He says: Month-old mail is worse than no mail. He'd rather get no letters, would rather not write what will probably not be true by the time it arrives. She thinks this is a little harsh. She would take any mail over no mail, but defers to him in this, and doesn't mention it to her lab technician friends with whom—when she stays in town after work for a movie or a fireworks display—she is trying to have a normal summer. When they ask after him, she smiles and shrugs, meaning, what can you say about someone who'd spend half a summer with monkeys? If she confessed that she never hears from him, they would point out that not writing at all isn't logical, as if she should have just told him that, as if they didn't know how rarely the logical thing is what you do. The Indians and Filipinos all have unhelpful stories of husbands who went off and started second families somewhere else. She knows he will call when he gets to San Juan, and that is, in fact, what happens.

By now she is used to his homecomings, and can get through them if she remembers not to expect any more than this: a certain distance, forgetfulness—that is, he seems to forget who she is and treats her with the dutiful politeness he must have shown whoever sat beside him on the plane ride home. She thinks they should hire an expert to repatriate *him*; but really, she is that expert. She knows what to cook: simple meals, no meat for a while. She could write a cookbook for women whose lovers have lived exclusively among animals. She knows to wait a day for each week he's been gone before thinking he doesn't love her, but even so, even knowing this, she'll still think he doesn't love her, and then *she* will forget,

forget what grace she has, drop things in the kitchen, forget where the holes in the lawn are, and trip and fall.

She expects this, she is prepared for it, but not for the man who gets out of his car and walks up her drive after two months in Puerto Rico. Something about him is different, he has lost weight. His body make a funny angle with the ground, forcing her to see pictures she'd rather not imagine: him hunkering, swinging his arms, screeching monkey talk about food. This is not how she wants to think about him, not ever, and especially not now, as he holds her, a little stiffly, so that she feels silly for hugging him, sees it anthropologically, really no different from jumping and clacking her teeth. Soon he lets her go, making such an effort to look into her eyes that she cannot look back, but only at his hands, hovering disappointedly in the air near her arms.

She offers him a beer but he doesn't want beer. Wine? He refuses. He doesn't want water, doesn't want juice. He isn't hungry. Banana? she says, holding up a bunch. That's not funny, he says, and heads out to the garden before she can warn him that the deer have eaten everything. Soup boils on the stove, she has to turn it down, has to taste it, has to splash soup on her shirt, rub soap in the stain, put water on it, change her shirt. Already she knows to watch for holes in the lawn, so she is tiptoeing, creeping up on him, and so is witness to the most extraordinary sight. Not six feet from him, a doe is grazing what's left of the pepper plants.

He will not eat dinner. He says he ate on the plane, ate something at his apartment. But what could have lasted in his apartment for two months? She has made him fresh corn chowder, broiled swordfish, red potatoes, sliced cucumbers with soy sauce and sesame oil, but she can't eat much either. She does dishes, they go for a walk up the road. By now he has been in her house six hours. Then they go to bed. He keeps turning her, he will only make love to her from behind. She knows not to turn and look, it would be awful to see how surprised he'd be to see her face. And anyway, she prefers it this way: he can't see she is crying. Later they lie there, not talking. She thinks he is totally gone, gone crazy, or worse, is going to tell her he's fallen in love with a monkey.

After a while he says he is sorry. He lies on his back and tells the ceiling that he is having a very bad time. He says what he found in Puerto Rico were forty or fifty monkeys, mostly adults—strong, unpredictable, destructive. First they harassed, then actually attacked a couple of workers building the plant, a couple of monkeys were shot before he was called in. They moved the monkeys in cages on pickup trucks: it was like the aftermath of a war, like some Hollywood epic retreat scene, complete with the bloody bandages. He says everyone knows stories about animal populations that just didn't make it, didn't adapt. He had never seen this himself, but there was something about these monkeys that made him think of it right away.

At first he kept them in cages. He let them watch him gathering food, picking the bananas and breadfruit he then left within their reach. The monkeys picked the bananas up and looked at them and dropped them. They stayed on a kind of hunger strike for a week. Finally he gave up, maybe they needed to gather the food themselves. So he let them out of the cages, but now *he* had to be in a cage, for his own protection. Getting them out, and him in, was a complicated maneuver, but he did it, and still the monkeys wouldn't forage, wouldn't eat.

After two weeks he could see that they'd gotten thinner. He began eating like crazy, bananas, bananas, bananas, showing them how it was done, but they knew that. They didn't want it. Another two weeks and the monkeys were very skinny, but there was nothing he could do, no one was going to force-feed them. Hospitalize them? Hook them all up to IVs? He began writing letters—Help, the monkeys are starving—mailing them out with the helicopters that dropped him extra food. And now he could see the monkeys getting dull and slack and sleepy; their fur was beginning to fall out. But maybe they were sneaking something at night, because it all happened so slowly, the whole thing took longer than he could believe.

Toward the end he thought of getting the trucks back and trucking them into the city and letting the monkeys die in the middle of downtown San Juan. But what would that have accomplished, except maybe scaring some children and getting him and the starving monkeys thrown in jail? So he stayed out in the jungle until they died. The children and the old ones went first. It took days, it was awful, bodies everywhere, like some nightmare monkey Jonestown. After he'd buried them all, he went into town. It was in San Juan that he realized he had stopped eating. He didn't—still doesn't—remember when he last ate. When he tries to eat, his throat clenches and he thinks he is going to choke.

Neither of them sleeps all night, though they both pretend. She wonders if monkeys ever pretend to sleep. She thinks of how once, long ago, a lover left her for someone else, a friend, a woman who used to visit them, and how the worst thing was wondering if the best way to win him back was to be more or less like that friend. What she feels now is so similar; she thinks: Should I be more human or more monkey?

In the morning she says she has a favor to ask him. She's read that the best thing to do with the garden would be to turn the ground over now, stockpile manure and lay it on before fall, before the snow. She has arranged with a neighbor to borrow his pickup, and a farmer just down the road has said they can have some manure from his barn. Will he help her while he is here?

She has given this a lot of thought, so it is not nearly as weird as it might seem, asking a lover who's just come home after two months to help you go get cowshit. She has found that chores like this—simple, physically demanding tasks connected unquestionably to survival—seem to do him good when he returns. The quickest recovery he ever made was one winter after he'd been with the elk: she got him to go out and split most of a cord of wood. Plus, this time she can't help hoping that her planning for seasons ahead will make him think well of her, see in her the best of human intelligence and animal instinct combined.

He says that he would be glad to help. He even makes a joke of being back twenty-four hours and already shoveling shit. She sees this as a good sign. She makes a point of how he has old clothes—boots, overalls, a shirt—stored in the front hall closet. Look, she says, your stuff. It takes some restraint not to ask if he's sure he doesn't want breakfast.

They drive to the farm. The farmer shows them where to

find the manure. They back the truck up to the barn door and start shoveling. They haven't worked long, a few minutes perhaps, but already this job they are doing together—efficiently, wordlessly—is making her feel more hopeful.

Then he sticks his pitchfork into the pile and exposes a nest of wriggling pink creatures, no bigger than a finger, blind, squirming and squealing in terror. What are they? Newborn mice? Impossibly tiny pigs? Surely he knows, but doesn't say; and suddenly she feels so distant from him that she can't even ask. She thinks she may always remember these creatures and never know what they were. He throws a ragged slab of manure back on top of the nest, gently tamps it down so the animals are covered, then goes out and sits in the truck. In a little while she joins him, he guns the engine, and they leave. She wonders how she will explain this the next time she sees the farmer.

At home she makes coffee. He puts his hands around the cup but doesn't drink. Through the window, she can see the pickup, the few clumps of manure still unloaded in back. Perfect, she thinks. He tells her he can't be with her, can't be with anyone now. He says it isn't fair to her, he is in terrible shape. He means it, he talks without stopping, without leaving her any silences in which to wedge an offer of patience or of help. Then he gets in his car and drives off.

She sits quietly for a while, wondering if, and how much, she should worry about him. Starving yourself is serious business. But then she thinks: He won't starve, he'll be all right, he is an expert on survival. This makes her feel slightly worse—does this mean she would rather he go crazy than just not love her? And *this* makes her think she deserves what has happened: she has not loved him unselfishly, or enough.

Now she is sorry she has taken this week off from work. She had imagined them spending it together. She would be better off in the lab, distracted, but she has told her friends at work he is coming home. If she cancels her vacation and goes in, she'll have to talk about him.

The first day of vacation she goes to the store and buys lots of food. After that she stays home. She decides not to call him. Instead she will make a list of things to remember to tell him, things that happen to her. Then she'll have the list if he calls.

At the end of the week he still hasn't called, so she decides to call *him*. She picks up the phone and as she dials, reads the list:

1. A flock of geese flew overhead and she thought it was barking dogs.

2. In the grocery store, she overheard one teenage mother telling another how, the first year after her kid was born, she rented a trailer from an old guy who had put an electronic bug zapper right outside her bedroom window. The purple light and the zapping kept waking up the baby. She kept turning the light off, but the landlord kept sneaking back over and turning it on, and finally they had an argument and he evicted her.

3. After that trip to the grocery store, she stopped going out, and spent the rest of her vacation in bed. She ate in bed, didn't bathe, watched a lot of TV. Her favorite part of the day was the early morning, before she was fully awake.

She would put her head under the covers, where it was warm and smelled of her body, and she breathed in the smell, with its edge of the zoo, a little bit like his smell.

She reads through the list again. She puts down the phone. She thinks: I have nothing to tell him that isn't about animals.

ELECTRICITY

Anita sails the baby over her head. "Earth to Spaceship Bertie," she says. "Earth to Spaceship Bertie. Can you read me?"

The baby's laugh sounds forced, like Johnny Carson's when he's blown a joke. Last week she caught Bertie practicing smiles in the mirror over his crib, phony social smiles for the old ladies who goo-goo him in the street, noticeably different from his real smile. It occurs to her that the baby is embarrassed for her. Lately she's often embarrassed for herself. This feeling takes her back fifteen years to her early teens, when she and her parents and her younger sister Lynne used to go places —Jones Beach, Prospect Park—and she'd see groups of kids her own age. At the time she had felt that being with her family made her horribly conspicuous; now she realizes that it probably made her invisible.

The house is quiet. Now since she's back is the first time Anita can remember being in her parents' home without the television going. She thinks of the years her father spent trailing her and Lynne from room to room, switching lights off behind them, asking who they thought was paying the electric bills. Yet he never turned the TV off; he'd fall asleep to the *Late Show*. Now the TV is dark, the house is lit up like a birthday cake, and her father is down in the finished basement, silenced by the acoustical ceiling as he claps his hands, leaps into the air, and sings hymns in praise of God and the Baal Shem Tov.

In the morning, when Anita's father goes off to the *bet hamidrash*, the house of study, Anita and her mother and the baby watch *Donahue*. Today the panel is made up of parents whose children have run away and joined cults. The week Anita came home, there was a show about grown children moving back in with their parents. It reminds Anita of how in high school, and later when she used to take acid, the radio always seemed to play oddly appropriate songs. Hearing the Miracles sing "What's So Good about Goodbye?" when she was breaking up with a boyfriend had made her feel connected with lovers breaking up everywhere. But now she hates to think that her life is one of those stories that make Donahue go all dewy-eyed with concern.

The twice-divorced mother of a Moonie is blaming everything on broken homes. "Don't you ever become a Moonie," Anita whispers, pressing her lips against the back of the baby's neck. Another mother is describing how her daughter calls herself Prem Ananda, wears only orange clothes, has married a boy the guru's chosen for her, and, with her doctorate in philosophy, works decorating cakes in the ashram bakery.

"Cakes?" says Anita's mother. "That's nothing. Only my Sam waits till he's fifty-seven to join a cult. After thirty-three years of marriage, he'll only make love through a hole in the sheet."

"A hole in the sheet?" Repeating this, Anita imagines Donahue repeating it, then realizes: incredibly, she and her mother have never talked about sex. Not ever. Imagining her mother on Donahue, Anita sees only close-ups, because if the camera pulled back, it would see up her mother's housedress to where the pale veined thighs dimple over the tops of her support hose.

Anita goes over and hugs her mother so hard that Bertie, squeezed between them, squawks like one of his bath toys. The baby starts to cry, her mother starts to cry, and Anita, not knowing what else to do, presses Bertie against her mother and pats and rubs them as if trying to burp both of them at once.

Anita takes nothing for granted. When she lifts her foot to take a step, she no longer trusts the ground to be there when she puts it down. She used to say that you could never really tell about people; now she knows it's true. She never once doubted that Jamie loved her, that he wanted the baby. When he came to visit her and Bertie in the hospital and began crying, she was so sure it was from happiness that she literally did not hear him say he'd fallen in love with somebody else.

She'd made him repeat it till he was almost shouting and she remembered who this Lizzie was: another lawyer in his office. At a garden party that summer Lizzie had asked to touch Anita's belly.

Just as Jamie was offering to move out of the house they had rented for its view, for their vision of children standing at the Victorian Bay window watching boats slip up the Hudson, a nurse wheeled the baby in, in a futuristic clear plastic cart.

"Spaceship Bertie," said Jamie.

Anita's sister Lynne says that men do this all the time: Jamie's acting out his ambivalence about fatherhood, his jealousy of the mother-infant bond. This sounds to Anita like something from Family Circle or Ladies' Home Journal. Lynne has read those magazines all her life, but now that she's going for her master's in women's studies, she refers to it as "keeping up." Lynne can't believe that Anita never had the tiniest suspicion. A year ago, Anita would have said the same thing, but now she knows it's possible. Whenever she thinks about last summer, she feels like a Kennedy-assassination buff examining the Zapruder film. But no matter how many times she rewinds it, frame by frame, she can't see the smoking gun, the face at the warehouse window. All she sees is that suddenly, everyone in the car starts moving very strangely.

Anita's mother believes her. Overnight, her husband turned into a born-again Hasid. Perhaps that's why she hardly sounded surprised when on the day she and Anita's father were supposed to drive up to Nyack to see the baby, Anita called to say that she and Bertie were coming to Brooklyn. Over the phone, her mother had warned her to expect changes. Daddy wasn't himself. No, he wasn't sick. Working too hard as usual, but otherwise fine. Her tone had suggested something shameful. Had he, too, fallen in love with somebody else?

Pulling into her parents' driveway, Anita thought: He looks the same. He opened the door for her and waited while she unstrapped Bertie from his car seat, then sidestepped her embrace. He'd never been a comfortable hugger, but now she missed his pat-pat-pat. She held Bertie out to him; he shook his head.

"Bertie, this is your grandpa," she said. "Grandpa, this is Bertie."

"Has he been circumcised?" asked her father.

"Of course," said Anita. "Are you kidding? My doctor did it in the hospital."

"Then we'll have to have it done again," said her father. "By a mohel."

"Again!" yelled Anita. "Are you out of your mind?"

Attracted by the noise, her mother came flying out of the house. "Sam!" She grabbed the baby from Anita. "Can't you see she's upset?"

The commotion had comforted Anita. Everything was familiar—their voices, the pressure of her mother's plump shoulder pushing her into the house, the way she said, "Coffee?" before they'd even sat down.

"I'll get it," said Anita. "You hold the baby." But her mother headed her off at the kitchen door.

"It's arranged a little different now," she explained. "Those dishes over there by the fridge are for meat. These here by the stove are for milk."

That night they couldn't eat till her father had blessed the half grapefruits, the maraschino cherries, the boiled flank steak, the potatoes and carrots, the horseradish, the unopened jar of applesauce, the kosher orange gelatin with sliced bananas. During the meal, Bertie began to fuss, and Anita guided his head up under her shirt.

"Is it all right if the baby drinks milk while I eat meat?" she asked. Her mother laughed.

"Edna," said her father, "don't encourage her."

Bertie cried when Anita tried to set him down, so she was left alone with her father while her mother did the dishes.

"What *is* this?" she asked him. "You never went to *shul* in your life. Aunt Phyllis and Uncle Ron didn't speak to us for a year because on the Saturday of Cousin Simon's bar mitzvah, you *forgot*—you said—and took us all to Rip Van Winkle's Storybook Village."

"I did forget." Her father laughed. "Anyhow, we didn't miss anything. Simon was bar-mitzvahed in the Reform temple. The church."

"The church!" repeated Anita. "Dad, what's the story?"

"The story, Anita?" Her father took a deep breath. Then he said:

"Once upon a time, a jeweler was taking the subway home to East Flatbush from his shop on Forty-sixth Street. At Nostrand, he finally got a seat and opened his *Post* when he heard loud voices at the far end of the car. Looking up, he saw three Puerto Rican kids in sneakers, jeans, and hot pink silk jackets which said 'Men Working' on the fronts, backs, and sleeves. When he realized that the jackets had been stitched together from the flags Con Ed put up near excavations, he found this so interesting that it took him a while to notice that the kids had knives and were working their way through the car, taking money and jewelry from the passengers and dropping them into a bowling bag. Then he thought: Only in New York do thieves wear clothes which glow in the dark. The boys didn't seem to be hurting anyone, but it still didn't make the jeweler comfortable. He thought: Is this how it happens? One night you pick the wrong subway car, and bingo! you're an item in the morning paper.

"Halfway down the car, they reached an old lady who started to scream. Then suddenly, the lights began to flash on and off in a definite pattern: three long blinks, three short blinks, three long blinks. By the fourth SOS the muggers had their noses pressed against the door, and when it opened at the station, they ran. 'Thank God, it's a miracle!' cried the old lady.

"Meanwhile the jeweler had his head between his knees. He was trying to breathe, thinking he must have been more scared than he'd known. Then he looked up and saw a young Hasidic man watching him from across the aisle.

" 'It wasn't a miracle,' said the Hasid. 'I did it. Follow me out at the next stop.'

"Normally, this jeweler wasn't the type to follow a Hasid out onto the Eastern Parkway station. But all he could think of was, had his wallet been stolen, he'd have had to spend all the next day at the Motor Vehicles Bureau replacing his license and registration. He felt that he owed somebody something, and if this Hasid was taking credit, keeping him company was the least he could do.

"On the platform, the Hasid pointed to a bare light bulb and said, 'Look,' The light blinked on and off. Then he waved at a buzzing fluorescent light. It blinked too. 'I lied before,' said the Hasid. 'It wasn't my doing. Everything is the rebbe's. . . .' "

Anita's father stopped when her mother came in, drying her hands. "Bertie!" Anita's mother cried, picking the baby up and waltzing him into the kitchen. "Don't listen to this nonsense! A whole life ruined for one blinky light bulb!"

"It wasn't the light," said Anita's father.

Anita wanted to ask if his story really happened or if he'd made it up as a metaphor for what happened. She thought: Something must have happened. In the old days, her father didn't make up stories. But she forgot her questions when she heard her mother in the kitchen singing "Music, Music, Music" to Bertie, singing "Put another nickel in, in the nickelodeon," sounding just like Teresa Brewer.

Now, five months later, watching the parents of cult members on Donahue, Anita decides that her father's story left out all the important parts. Such as: why he really joined. There's no overlooking the obvious reasons: old age, sickness, death. If they'd been Protestant and he'd converted to Catholicism, no one would have wondered why.

She remembers a weekend this past summer when Jamie was away on business—with Lizzie, she thinks now—and her

parents came up to see her. Her father drove her to the supermarket to shop for their visit and for Jamie's return. At the
checkout stand, the kid who packed their order insisted, over
her father's protests, on wheeling the cart out and loading
the bags into their—the old man's, the pregnant woman's—
car. Like her father, Anita was angry at the kid. Couldn't he
see that her father could have done it? Not for nothing did he
swim fifteen laps at the JCC pool every Sunday morning. But
the crazy thing was, for the whole way home, Anita was mad at
her father.

Her father is still in shape. And despite all the rushing to
shul every morning and from there to work, he seems pretty
relaxed. What's hurting her family, Anita decides, is the un-
predictability, the shaky sense that everyone is finally unreliable.
What's bothering her mother is that the man she's shared her
bed with for thirty-three years has suddenly and without warning rolled to the opposite side. She must wonder if the sheet
with the hole in it has been there all along.

Anita wants to tell her mother that there's no guarantee;
you can't know anything about anyone. She wants to ask:
What's so strange about a man wanting to sing and dance his
way into heaven? But if they've never even talked about sex,
how can they talk about this?

Anita bundles Bertie up in so many layers that he does look
like a spaceman, and takes him to the library. On the subway,
she notices that the lights flash on and off. The train is almost
empty and she thinks about muggers in hot pink Con Ed

jackets, but feels that Bertie is a kind of protection. Babies are unpredictable, like crazy people; she's heard you can sometimes scare muggers away by pretending to be crazy.

The librarians in the Judaica section eye Bertie so suspiciously that he exhausts himself trying to charm them and falls asleep in Anita's arms. Juggling baby and purse, she pulls out some reference books on Hasidism and sits down.

She's surprised at how much she already knows, what she has picked up from growing up in New York, from college, reading, and sheer osmosis. She starts Martin Buber's *Tales of the Hasidim*, then decides she must have read it or else heard the stories somewhere. She thinks of Jamie's friend Ira who'd visited once a year from his Orthodox commune in Cambridge, bringing his own food in an Empire Kosher Poultry shopping bag. She can't remember him telling stories.

For information about her father's sect, she's directed to the microfilm section. The librarian hands her a flat box, then seeing that it's impossible for her to thread the machine while holding Bertie, gives her a sour smile and does it for her.

For some reason, they've microfilmed whole editions of the city papers. Anita likes flipping back through the pages; it's like reading a story when you already know the end, only eerier. Meanwhile she learns that fifteen years ago, her father's group came from Hungary via Israel to their present home in Brooklyn. In the centerfold of the *Daily News*, there's a photo of the rebbe walking from Kennedy airport to Brooklyn because his plane from Jerusalem had landed on the Sabbath, when he wasn't allowed to ride. Taken at night, the picture is blurred, hard to read. The rebbe is all white hair and white beard, Mr.

Natural in a beaver hat. On the next page is an ad for leather boots from Best and Co.—thirty dollars, fifteen years ago, an outrageously low price.

Ironically, the reason Anita can't concentrate is that she's being distracted by the noise from the Mitzvahmobile parked on Forty-second Street, blaring military-sounding music from its loudspeakers. She pictures the Hasidim darting from one pedestrian to another, asking, "Excuse me, are you Jewish?"

One afternoon, not long after she and Jamie first fell in love, they were approached by the Mitzvahmobilers, and Jamie said yes, he was Jewish. They dragged him—literally dragged him—into the trailer. The weather was nice, and nothing in those days seemed like an imposition, so Anita had waited on the library steps till Jamie emerged, looking pale.

Apparently, the Hasidim had tried to teach him how to lay tefillin, but he just couldn't get the hang of it. He froze, his hands wouldn't work. Finally they gave up. They put the phylacteries in his hands, then covered his hands with theirs and just held them, one on his forehead, and one on his arm near his heart.

On Friday nights, Anita's father sleeps at the bet hamidrash so he won't have to travel on the Sabbath, and her sister Lynne comes for dinner.

As children, Anita and Lynne fought, as their mother says, tooth and nail. Now it's simpler: they love one another—so Anita feels disloyal for thinking that Lynne is just like Valerie Harper playing Rhoda. But it's true, and it's not just the curly hair, the tinted glasses, the running shoes, and the tight designer jeans. It's Lynne's master's thesis, "The Changing Role of Women as Reflected in Women's Magazines, 1930–1960." It's her job as a social worker in a family-planning clinic and her boyfriend Arnie, who's almost got his degree as a therapist and is already practicing on the Upper West Side.

Lynne and Anita kiss hello. Then Lynne puts her arms around their mother, who's stirring something at the stove, and hugs her for so long that Anita starts feeling uncomfortable. Finally she zeroes in on Bertie, ensconced in his yellow plastic recliner chair on the kitchen table.

"Look how he holds his head up!" says Lynne.

Bertie's been holding his head up since he was two weeks old, and Lynne's seen it, but Anita refrains from pointing this out. Together they set the table, then Lynne pulls her into a corner and asks what she hears from Jamie.

"Oh, he's coming to see Bertie tomorrow."

Lynne stares at Anita, trying to ascertain if this "means" anything. Then she gets her purse and starts rummaging around. She takes out a tortoiseshell case, brushes tobacco dust off it, and gives it to Anita, who knows what it is before she opens it: eye shadow, a palette of different colors.

"Thanks," says Anita. The gift moves her and reminds her of what she's always known: her sister is less of a feminist or a Rhoda than a real magazine reader, a girl who believes in her heart that eye shadow can change your luck.

For Lynne, their mother has cooked the same company dinner she made when Anita first came home. But without their father's blessing, the meat tastes greasy, the potatoes lukewarm; the gelatin has a rubbery skin. His absence should free them, thinks Anita, but he's all they talk about, in voices so low he might as well be downstairs.

With Lynne's coaching, their mother talks, and Anita sees she's been wrong: her mother's unhappiness isn't philosophical, it's practical. Imagine being forced to start keeping a kosher home at the age of fifty-three! Two sets of dishes! The doctor says salting the meat is bad for her heart. The smallest details of life now have rules which Sam won't let her break; she has to take the train to Essex Street to buy special soap for him.

If it gets much worse, Lynne suggests, she might consider a trial separation.

"Who would it help?" their mother asks. "Would it make me happier? Would it make Daddy happier?"

"I doubt it," says Anita.

"What would make me happy," their mother says, "is for Daddy to turn back into his normal self."

Anita wonders what would make her happy. Lately she's not sure. Bertie makes her happy, but it seems important to remember: he'll grow up and leave her. If you can count on anything, she thinks, it's that.

She senses that Lynne is talking less about happiness than about punishment. Lynne feels that their father is responsible for their mother's troubles, just as Jamie is for hers. Anita thinks that no one's to blame for her parents' situation; and in her own case, she's partly at fault.

Her first mistake was to gain so much weight when she was pregnant. Why should Jamie have faith she'd lose it when her own doctor didn't? Now she has, but, clearly, it's too late.

Her second mistake was to quit her job, even if it was the lowest editorial job in the world, the slush pile at *Reader's*

Digest. Most of the submissions were for "The Most Unforgettable Character I've Ever Met," and most of these had never
done one unforgettable thing except die slowly of some horrible
cancer. Jamie liked hearing about them; he said they made him
feel better about *his* day. And after she quit and took to reading
long novels—anything, so long as it went on for more than
four hundred pages—it wasn't the same. She'd try to tell
Jamie about the Baron Charlus or Garp's mother, and he'd
be staring past her. Once, to test him, she said, "My doctor said
it's going to be triplets," and he just kept gazing beyond her
out the dark kitchen window at the lights moving slowly up
the Hudson.

Which reminds her of her third mistake: they never argued.
Lynne, who fights with Arnie over every little thing, has told
her that she and Jamie were afraid of their anger. Maybe so.
Even when Jamie told her he was leaving, Bertie was there,
listening to what for him was their first conversation. How
could they have fought?

Anita wonders what happened to that part of her that used
to fight tooth and nail with Lynne. She imagines Jamie and
Lizzie litigating over every avocado in the supermarket. It's the
only way she can stand thinking of him in the supermarket
with somebody else.

Once, visiting friends in Berkeley, Anita and Jamie went to
an all-night supermarket for orange juice. They took a joint for
the ride and got so stoned that, when they got there, they
couldn't move. They just stood near the vegetable bins, talking, laughing, marveling over the vegetables, those California
vegetables!

Once more, Anita feels like she's watching the Zapruder film. She's the only assassination buff who can't even handle a magnifying glass, who wouldn't know a smoking gun if she saw one.

Anita's wasted the morning trying to imagine her conversation with Jamie. She's afraid she'll have nothing interesting to say. She blames this on living in her parents' house, where nothing interesting ever happens. She feels that living there marks her as a boring person with no interesting friends she could have stayed with. But that's not true. She and Bertie would have been welcome in the editing room of Irene's SoHo loft, on the couch in Jeanie's Park Slope floor through. But being home is easier, she doesn't have to be a good guest. If Bertie cries at night, her mother comes in and offers to sing him Teresa Brewer.

One thing she could tell Jamie is what she's noticed at the Pathmark: more and more people seem to be buying huge quantities of specialty items, whole shopping carts full of apricot yogurt, frozen tacos, Sprite in liter plastic jugs. She's heard that American families hardly ever sit down to dinner together. So who knows, maybe there are millions of people out there, each eating only one thing. She could tell him how she took Bertie to the park to see some other babies. He slept the whole time, leaving her with the other mothers, none of whom even smiled at her. At one point, a little boy threw sand at a little girl. The girl's mother ran over, grabbed the boy's ankles, and turned him upside down. Anita expected coins to rain out of his pockets like in the movies, but none did. After a while, the boy's mother came over, and, instead of yelling at the woman who was shaking her upside-down son, said, "I'm glad it's you and not me." Anita felt as if she'd stumbled in on a game already in progress, like polo or a new kind of poker with complicated rules which no one would stop to explain.

But the last thing she wants is to sound like some pitiful housewife drifting back and forth between the supermarket and the playground. She wonders what sort of lawyer Lizzie is. Corporate taxes, she hopes, but fears it's probably the most interesting cases: mad bombings, ax murders, billion-dollar swindles.

She's tempted to tell Jamie about her father, how for a week or so last month he'd been instructed by his rebbe: instead of saying grace, he should clap his hands whenever the spirit of thanksgiving moved him. In the hour and a half it took to eat —with her father dropping his silverware, clapping, shutting his eyes as if smelling something sweet—Anita tried to predict these outbursts, but couldn't; she thought of the retarded people one heard sometimes in movie theaters, shouting out randomly, for no reason. She could tell Jamie how her father came home in a green velvet Tyrolean hat with a feather; apparently, the rebbe had given out dozens of hats to illustrate his sermon: the righteous man must climb this world like a mountain.

But she knows that telling Jamie would only make her angry at him for not being around tomorrow when she'll need to tell him the next installment. Nor does it make her happy right now to think that Jamie knows her father well enough to know that in the old days, he wouldn't have been caught dead in a Tyrolean hat.

The obvious subject is Bertie. Everything he does interests her; she thinks he's a genius. Why can't she tell Jamie about his practiced smiles, about his picking up his own Cheerios? Why? Because what could be more pitiful than thinking that anyone cares if your five-month-old can pick up his own Cheerios?

Bertie's victory over Cheerios should be their victory. In stead, she can hardly talk about Bertie; it's as if she's accusing Jamie. Bertie should be the mortar cementing them; as it is, he's part of the wall.

When Jamie rings the doorbell, Anita half hopes that Bertie, who hasn't seen his father for two weeks, will not recognize him and scream. Bertie looks at Jamie, then at Anita, then at Jamie, then smiles a smile which anyone could tell is his real one.

Anita's mother says, "Jamie! There's apple cake in the fridge if you kids get hungry." Then she backs out of the room. It's so uncomfortable they could be high-schoolers dating—except for the presence of Bertie and the fact that Anita and Jamie didn't know each other in high school.

"Can we go for a walk somewhere?" Jamie is staring to the side of Anita's head, at Bertie. Anita feels as if he's asking Bertie out and is one of those guys who's scared to be alone with his date. She's the friend he drags along, the chaperone.

"Sure," says Anita. Bertie's wriggling so hard his feet jam

halfway down the legs of his snowsuit and Anita has to thread them through. She knows she's making herself look incompetent, making the process of dressing Bertie look harder than it is.

On the way to the park she can't think of anything to say. She doesn't want to discuss specialty items at the Pathmark or the upside-down boy. Of course she's done this before, rehearsed whole conversations that turned out to be inappropriate. But never with Jamie.

The playground is chilly, almost deserted. In one corner, two five-year-old boys are playing soccer while their parents— all four of them in ponytails—hunker on the ground, passing a joint. There's a dressed-up Orthodox family sitting in a row on a bench. By the swings, a young mother says to her daughter, "Okay, ten more pushes and we're going home." And finally there are some boys—ten, eleven, twelve—playing very hard and punishingly on the jungle gym and slide, as if it's the playground equipment's fault that they've grown too big for it.

"When is Bertie going to be old enough for the slide?" asks Jamie.

"Tomorrow," says Anita.

The mother by the swings counts to ten, and when the little girl says "Ten more!" grabs her daughter's hand and pulls her out of the park. Jamie sits down on one of the swings and stretches his arms out for Bertie. Holding the baby on his lap, Jamie pushes off. Anita can't look till she reassures herself: she trusts Jamie that much—not to drop Bertie. She sits on the other swing and watches Bertie, who is leaning forward to see where they're going before they get there.

"Look how he holds his head up," says Jamie. "That's my boy."

"He's been doing that for four months," says Anita.

Jamie trails his long legs in the sand and stops with a bump. "Anita," he says, "just what am I supposed to do? What do you want?"

Anita wonders what she does want. She's not sure she wants to be back with Jamie. Bertie or no Bertie, it's too late. Something's happened that can't be fixed. Basically, she wants what her mother wants: for everything to be the way it was before everything changed.

"I want to know one thing," she says. "Remember that garden party at Mel's?"

"What about it?" says Jamie.

Anita remembers a buffet of elegant, salty things—sun-dried tomatoes, smoked salmon—which by then she wasn't allowed to eat. "I want to know if you and Lizzie were already . . ." She thinks: If a woman could walk clear across a party to feel her lover's wife's belly, her lover's unborn child inside it, well then, you really can't know anything about people.

Jamie says, "Of course not," but in a tone that makes Anita suspect it began at that party, or thereabouts. She wonders: Did their fingers brush accidentally over a Lebanese olive? A long look near the pesto and sour-cream dip?

"It wasn't Lizzie." Jamie's swinging again, distractedly. "It wasn't you."

"Who was it?" she says. "Don't blame Bertie, he wasn't born yet."

"It wasn't the baby. It was me. Listen—" Jamie stops himself by grabbing the chain on her swing together with his. The seats tilt together crazily. "When I was in the seventh grade, there was a kid in my class named Mitchell Pearlman. One day we got to talking about our dads, and Mitchell said that his was a photographer. He'd been everywhere, done everything. Had he fought with the Mau Maus? Sure. Sipped tea with Queen Elizabeth? Of course. Lived with the Eskimos, crossed the Sahara on a camel? You bet.

"Naturally we thought he was lying till we went to his house for his birthday. The minute we met Mitchell Pearlman's father—mustache, jeans, big silver belt buckle—we began to think Mitchell was telling the truth. After the cake and ice cream, his father brought out the pictures of himself in front of the igloo, the camel, arm in arm with Jomo Kenyatta, dandling the baby Prince Charles on his knee. And for months after that, for years, I hated my own father. I wouldn't speak to him."

"So?" says Anita. "I don't get it."

"So, when Bertie was born, I suddenly thought: In a couple of years, he'll be me in the seventh grade. And I'll be my father. And he'll go out and find his own Mitchell Pearlman's father. And he'll hate me. I thought: We've made a terrible mistake! We should have waited to have Bertie till I was Mitchell Pearlman's father! Does this make any sense?" There are tears in Jamie's eyes.

Anita thinks: Not much. For one thing, the chronology's wrong. Jamie fell in love *before* Bertie was born. For another, Bertie isn't Jamie and Jamie isn't his father. Jamie's father owns a dry cleaners, while Jamie is a labor lawyer with interesting cases. She wants to shout at him that exchanging long looks with a lady lawyer over the pesto is nothing—nothing at all—like fighting with the Mau Maus. But she doesn't. She's beginning to see that her sister's right: this is something some men do. Jamie himself doesn't understand, any more than Mitchell Pearlman's father understood why he found it so easy to leave the wife and kids and take off across the Sahara.

She imagines Jamie ten years hence, taking Bertie out for the afternoon. He's one of those weekend fathers she never really noticed till she was pregnant, and then she saw them everywhere. She could always tell how uneasy it made them to take their kids places whole families went. Recently she read in the *Times*: there's a health club in Manhattan which, on Saturdays and Sundays, caters exclusively to single fathers and their children. Ten years from now, there will be hundreds of these places.

She imagines men and children lolling in a steamy pool, pumping exercycles, straining on Nautilus machines. There are no women in her vision, it's as if all the mothers have died of some plague. She hears the cries of the children, sees the shoulders of the fathers rounded as if from the weight of the children tugging their arms.

The only thing she can't picture is how Bertie will look in ten years' time.

For weeks, her father has been asking her to come to a service in his *shul*. "The worst that'll happen is that you'll have fun," he says. It's made Anita a little nervous, like having a Moonie ask her to go away for the weekend. But the day after Jamie's visit, she agrees. There's nothing but football on TV.

"Can me and Bertie sit in the same section?" she asks.

"Don't be smart," says her father.

When she comes downstairs in a turtleneck and good brown corduroy jeans, she sees him really suffering with embarrassment. She goes and changes into a long skirt from the back of her closet, Indian print from the sixties.

On the drive down Eastern Parkway, Anita and her father don't talk. Again she has the peculiar feeling of being on a date. There's not much traffic on this Sunday, and everything seems so slowed down that she's slow to notice: her father's whole driving style has changed. He used to zip around like a cabbie, teeth grinding, swerving, cursing. Now he keeps to his lane, he's got all the time in the world. His elbow is out the side window, and cold air is rushing into the car.

"Can you shut that?" says Anita. "The baby."

"Sure," says her father. "Sorry."

"What kind of service are we going to?"

"A wedding."

"Turn the car around," says Anita.

"Don't be stupid," says her father. "Would you have preferred a funeral? All right—next time, a funeral."

"What next time?" says Anita.

"You'll be interested," says her father. "The ceremony is outside, under the stars."

"Stars you can see from Crown Heights?" says Anita. "I'll be interested."

In the old days, her father used to start looking for parking places miles in advance. She remembers hours of accelerating, then falling forward as the brakes squealed in the search for a spot in Chinatown. Now as they pull up to the block in which hundreds of Hasidim are milling around, her father cruises smoothly into an empty space.

The short winter afternoon is darkening. The street lights come on. The air is crisp and clear. The men wear nearly identical black coats, the women's are of various subdued hues. Most of the women are in high, good leather boots which remind Anita of the ad on the microfilm. It's easy to spot the converts like her father in his fur-collared car coat, the young men in denim and down; it annoys her that several young women wear paisley skirts much like hers.

The crowd spills off the sidewalk, blocking the northbound lane, but the two cops parked in their squad car ignore it. Leaning on other cars, Puerto Rican kids in sweatshirts and down vests idly hump their girlfriends as they watch the Hasidim assemble. The wedding canopy is already up, held by four men who keep switching the pole from hand to hand so they can warm the free hand in their pockets.

Suddenly everyone's buzzing like bees. Anita's father leans forward and says, "The rebbe."

Anita stands on tiptoe. But from a quarter block away, the rebbe looks pretty much like the photo: Mr. Natural. That's another reason she could never join this sect: being female, she'd never get closer to the rebbe than this. She turns to say this to her father, but he's gone—drawn, she imagines, toward his rebbe.

The crowd buzzes again when the bride and groom appear. The bride's leaning on some women, the groom on some men. They both look ready to drop. When Anita gets a good look at the groom—gangly, skin the color of skim milk—she understands why the bride can hardly walk. How could anyone marry that?

Nearly rigid in his quilted snowsuit, Bertie's getting heavy. Anita holds him up though she knows he's too young to focus on the center of attention, too young to know there is a center. To Bertie, everything's the center: the scarf of the woman in front of him, his own inaccessible fist.

Anita thinks: the bride must be freezing. Maybe that's why she's so hunched over as the women lead her in circles around the groom. Under the veil, she could be anything—old, ugly, sick, some covered-up temple idol. No wonder the groom is so panicky!

Even with all the Hebrew prayers, the ceremony is over in no time. They always are, thinks Anita, except when people write their own. Real religions and even the state seem to know: if it drags on too long, somebody will faint. Anita and Jamie got married impulsively in a small town on the California-Nevada border. What she mostly remembers is sitting in a diner in Truckee, writing postcards to all their friends saying that she'd just been married in the Donner Pass by a one-armed justice of the peace.

Her thoughts are interrupted by cheers; the groom has broken the glass. Then bride and groom and wedding canopy

disappear in the crowd bearing them—and Anita and Bertie—
into the hall.

Just inside the door, the men and women peel off in opposite
directions. Anita follows the women into a large room with a
wooden dance floor surrounded by round tables, set with cen-
terpieces of pink carnations in squat crystal vases and group-
ings of ginger ale and seltzer bottles.

No one's saving places or jockeying to be near friends. The
ladies just sit. Anita stands for a minute or so, then sees two
women beckoning and patting the chair between them, so she
goes and sits down. She soon understands why the women have
found places so quickly: it doesn't matter where they sit, no
one stays put for more than two seconds. They kiss and gab,
then get up, sit next to a friend at another table, kiss and gab
some more. Meanwhile the waiters are weaving through with
bowls of hot soup, shouting to the women to get out of their
way. But no one's paying attention.

The woman to Anita's right is middle-aged and kind of
pretty. She's Mrs. Lesser. When the waiter brings Anita's
soup, Mrs. Lesser pushes it away so Anita won't spill it in her
struggle with Bertie's zipper.

"Your first baby?" asks Mrs. Lesser.

"Yes," says Anita.

"I had my first when I was sixteen. Can you believe I'm a
grandmother?"

Anita might not have thought it, but she can believe it; she
doesn't know quite what to say.

"Can you believe it?" Mrs. Lesser puts her big face near

Bertie's little one, and Bertie rewards her with his most radiant, sweetest, and most inauthentic social smile.

"Look at this baby smile!" Mrs. Lesser says to the whole table. "Look at this sweetheart!" It's Anita's introduction to the room at large, and all at once it's open season on Bertie. Mrs. Lesser gets up and someone else sits down and starts stroking Bertie's cheek.

These women have children and grandchildren of their own, thinks Anita. Why are they so interested? But they are, they're full of questions. How old is he? What's his name? Does he sleep through the night? Is he always so good?

Anita feels like Bertie's ventriloquist. She has to make an effort to speak in her normal voice as she says, "His name's Bertie. He's five months old. He can pick up his own Cheerios."

"Cheerios?" cry the women. "At five months? He's a genius!"

The partition separating the men's and women's sections stops a few feet from the ceiling. Anita's facing it when suddenly she sees three furry brown things fly up, then plummet, then fly again. Just as she figures out someone's juggling hats, she hears applause from the other side of the plywood.

With each course, a different woman is making Bertie smile and nibbling from whatever plate the waiter has put down. First comes stuffed derma, then a platter of thick roast beef, little round potatoes, canned peas. Anita picks up a forkful of peas. She isn't very hungry, it isn't very good. No one's eating much; even the fleshiest ladies are just tasting. But every woman who sits down offers to hold Bertie for Anita, or to cut her roast beef. They say to Bertie, "Too bad you can't eat roast beef, pussycat," and "Next year at this time you'll be munching little brown potatoes."

. . .

Slowly at first, the men begin dancing. Anita feels it through the floor before she hears it. Stamp, stamp. Soon the silverware is rattling, the peas are jumping on her plate. The stamping gets faster, there are shouts. Anita wonders if her father is dancing. Probably he is. The door between the two sections is open, children are running back and forth. No one would stop her from looking. But she doesn't, she just doesn't.

Singing, clapping, the men make their own music. The women have help. Two men come in with an accordion and a mandolin. The women dance sweetly in couples, a dance that seems part waltz, part foxtrot, part polka. Mrs. Lesser reappears, and when a sprightly gray-haired lady to the far side of her makes swaying motions with her arms, Mrs. Lesser says, "If you're asking, I'm dancing," and away they go. A tiny old woman approaches Anita and says, "Would the baby care to dance?"

All the women want to dance with Bertie. Young and old, they keep cutting in, passing him around. Anita catches glimpses of him, first with this one, then with that, sailing, swaying to the music, resting his cheek on their pillowy breasts. When Mrs. Lesser sits back down, she asks where the baby is.

"Dancing," says Anita.

Mrs. Lesser cranes her neck. "He's smiling," she says. "He's the belle of the ball!"

Suddenly there's a whoop from the other room, and Anita sees the groom's head and shoulders over the partition. From the angle of his head, the stricken expression, she knows that this is the part where the men hoist the groom up in a chair and dance. Then the women gather and raise the bride's chair. The music gets louder, and the women begin circling the bride, dancing with such intensity that Anita goes and finds Bertie and takes him back.

At last the bride's head is nearly touching the ceiling. Above the partition, she and the groom look at each other. Anita wants to study this look. She thinks it's something she should pay close attention to. But she's only half-watching. Mostly she's concentrating on not dropping Bertie, whom she's holding up above her head.

"Look, sweetheart," she's saying. "Look at the lady in the chair!"

Bertie sings when he nurses, a sweet satisfied gulping and humming high in his nose. That night, after the wedding, Anita falls asleep while he's nursing, and his song turns into the song in her dream.

In her dream, Bertie's singing "Music, Music, Music" just like Teresa Brewer. He's still baby Bertie, but he's up on stage, smiling one of his phony smiles, making big stagey gestures like Shirley Temple or those awful children in *Annie*. One of these gestures is the "okay" sign, thumb and forefinger joined. The circle his fingers make reminds her of the Buddha. It reminds her of a Cheerio.

Anita wakes up laughing, wondering how a little baby could know words like "nickelodeon." She gets up, and without detaching Bertie from her breast, slips a bathrobe over both of them and goes downstairs. Except for her parents' bedroom, where earlier she heard her mother preparing for sleep, every room is lit up. In the kitchen, light is shining from around the edges of the cellar door. Anita and Bertie go down.

Opening the door to the family room, she sees her father sitting cross-legged on the cork-tiled floor. His eyes are shut and tears are shining on his cheeks. But he's not so out of it that he doesn't hear her come in. Looking up, he seems frail and embarrassed, an old man caught doing something he's not supposed to do.

Anita wants to apologize and leave. Then it dawns on her that she's not down there to bother him. There's something she wants to ask, but she's not sure what it is. She wants to ask why all the lights in the house are always on. She wants to ask who he thinks is paying the electric bills.

Anita's father stands up and dries his eyes with his palm. Then he says, "Hold up your hand."

Anita holds up her hand and he lifts his, palm facing hers, a few inches away. He asks if she feels anything.

She feels something. A pressure.

She remembers how when she was in labor with Bertie, she held Jamie's hand. Just before the nurses let her start pushing, she turned to Jamie and said, "I don't think I can do this." "Sure you can," he said, and squeezed her hand so hard she'd thought it was broken. By the time it stopped hurting, the contraction was over and she knew she could go on. Now she sees that Jamie didn't mean to hurt her. He was scared too.

Her father's hand is still a few inches away, but its grip feels as tight as Jamie's. She can almost feel electrons jumping over the space between them, electricity drawing them as close as she is to Bertie, who just at that moment lets go of her breast and sits up, watching them.

EVERYDAY

DISORDERS

When Gilda tries to imagine what Phoebe Morrow looks like, she pictures Amelia Earhart in her rumpled jumpsuit, those fetching goggles and helmet rising straight from the cockpit, long scarf floating straight back, until Gilda realizes that what she's seeing isn't Phoebe or Amelia Earhart at all, but, rather, Snoopy as the Red Baron. Lately Gilda's been troubled by this confusion of images. This winter she reread *Madame Bovary*, and Emma's swoony romantic airs kept bringing to mind Miss Piggy. Gilda blames this on how much of the last dozen years she's spent among children. Childless women have other problems, she knows, but she's pretty sure that the inability to distinguish the mythic from the cartoon isn't one of them. When Phoebe Morrow aims her camera at the horizon, she's not seeing an untrustworthy line which may at any moment turn into a tightrope for Koko the Clown to bounce on; when Phoebe took those famous photographs of the dead Marines in Beirut, she knew she wasn't shooting GI Joe.

Making a square with her fingers, Gilda frames her living room to see what in that mass of discarded clothes and sports equipment and chewed-up baseball cards might catch Phoebe's eye. Nothing, she realizes, and anyway, Nathan's already taken that shot. Nathan's made his name as a chronicler of everyday disorder, so sometimes it seems unfair that he should chide Gilda for being, alternately, too fussy and not neat enough. The worst argument they ever had was years ago, when Gilda asked Nathan if he'd clean up the downstairs—in fact he *had* been cleaning, but the children were too much for them both—and he'd said, "After the revolution you'll be the commissar of cleanliness, the minister who makes sure that everyone keeps their houses neat and tidy." By now they know there won't be any revolution, not here in northern Pennsylvania, anyway, and if there is, they won't be the ones to lead it. Since then they've had more serious fights, meaner and closer to the bone. But the reason she still considers that one the worst is that whenever she straightens up—as she is doing now, as she does fairly often, to be sure—she remembers what

Nathan said, and it spoils her pleasure in the work and in the look of things when she's done.

Gilda's looking for reasons to be angry at Nathan because the real reason seems so meanspirited and small: she's upset that he's gotten Phoebe Morrow a one-year job at the college, that he's picking her up at the airport and they're headed back here for lunch. At times like this she feels like one of those wives who work to send their husbands through medical or law school and then the husbands take their fancy practices and split. It's not that Nathan's about to leave her—things feel solid enough, he's not looking for someone else—or that she's ever supported him, but rather that his whole career has been built on his photos of her and their family and their house. What cinched his reputation was that series he took when Gilda's grandfather came to live with them, that terrible year at the end of her grandfather's life; it seems incredible now that the first time she really knew Pop was dying was when she read it in a review of Nathan's show. Nathan's never understood why it bothered her so when critics wrote of Gilda's face as balancing on the border between the beautiful and the impossibly ugly. But all that, Gilda understands now, was nothing compared to how she's felt lately when Nathan, criticizing his own work, says it's all trivial, meaningless, small, come to nothing; Gilda can't help thinking he means her. She knows it's why he pressured his colleagues to hire Phoebe Morrow, who's been to Beirut, Nicaragua, Iraq, whose specialties are guerrilla encampments, free-fire zones, and risking her neck. Not only does Nathan admire Phoebe's work; he wishes he'd led her life.

That's what Gilda's thinking when the doorbell rings and why she has a rictus grin on her face and someone else's tight voice in her mouth as she says, "Nathan, sweetheart, why didn't you use your key?" What strikes Gilda right away is that Phoebe *does* look a bit like Amelia Earhart, that same clear wide forehead, those friendly wide-open eyes, and also a little—Gilda's veering towards the cartoon again—like Betty Boop. What Gilda has been hoping for, of course, was someone more serious-looking, and homelier. Phoebe's wearing a pink silk shirt, tight jeans, little heels. When Nathan introduces them, Phoebe grasps Gilda's hand in both of hers, and Gilda wonders how those delicate arms can possibly heft all that heavy camera equipment.

"Gilda?" Phoebe has enormous blue eyes and is shining them straight at Gilda. "Don't tell me. Your mother saw Rita Hayworth in *Gilda* right before you were born."

"You got it," says Gilda graciously, because she thinks she's scored one off Phoebe: lots of people—movie buffs and nearly everyone over thirty-five—say the same thing. Gilda glances at Nathan to see if he's noticed, but he's too busy looking for somewhere to put Phoebe's expensive-looking luggage. Then Phoebe says, "You know what I can't stop thinking about? Rita Hayworth having Alzheimer's. Forgetting all those beautiful nightgowns and how red her hair was and riding around in Ali Khan's fast cars and getting her picture taken kneeling on those messed-up satin sheets . . ."

Gilda, who's been half-poised for a retreat to the kitchen, turns and stops, and it's at this point that it occurs to her that she might actually *like* Phoebe Morrow. Not only has she been thinking, on and off for months and in much the same terms, about Rita Hayworth's Alzheimer's, but there's something about that kind of thinking—a frank taste for celebrity gossip combined with a certain way of paying attention to the world and in particular to those ironies so appalling they seem both predictable and ultimately bizarre—which appeals to her in people.

"As a matter of fact," Phoebe says, "I wanted to go out to wherever she is and take pictures—"

"That'd be a real change of pace for you," says Nathan with a kind of desperate hopefulness which suddenly makes Gilda think of how their youngest son Danny—for years, afraid of the water—would brighten when he heard the other kids deciding it was too cold for them to swim, too.

"But I didn't think I could handle it," says Phoebe, and then, noticing the surprise on both Gilda's and Nathan's faces, says, "It's easier taking pictures of dead people."

There's a silence during which Gilda thinks—and wonders if Nathan's thinking—of the bitter disagreement they had when Nathan wanted to take pictures of Gilda's grandfather in his coffin. Later, when Gilda was finally able to look at them, she understood that the photos were very moving and beautiful and really not ghoulish at all. Nevertheless, when she leafs through the book of Nathan's photos, as she still occasionally does, she finds herself skipping that page.

"You must be starving," she says to Phoebe. "Come on, let's eat."

It's only within the last year or so that Gilda's been able to set the table before guests arrive. She used to wait till they got there, then set out stacks of plates, silverware in a pile; it was a way of pretending she didn't care. All that casualness was planned; that's how nervous she is when strangers come to her house. Today she brings out an enormous tureen of hot mushroom soup she spent all yesterday making with heavy cream and mushrooms and fresh-grated nutmeg. She told herself she was giving the flavors an extra day to meld but the truth is, when she cooks the same day guests are coming she can't eat, can't even pretend; and though she explains all that, she often wonders if strangers suspect her of covering up some life-threatening appetite disorder.

"Hey," Nathan says, "this is unbelievably great," and Gilda thinks how like him that is. He's generous with everything— with praise, with blame, with enthusiasm, attention for the children. She wants to reach out and touch his hand, but finds it no easier now than it was twenty years ago when they first fell in love. Then it was shyness restraining her; now it's the tactlessness of indulging in that cozy married-couple stuff in front of the unattached.

"These are real mushrooms, aren't they?" says Phoebe. "I mean, fresh mushrooms, you must have made this from scratch." When Gilda nods, Phoebe says, "I've never had this before. Not real mushroom soup from scratch. Oh, Gilda, this is perfect, I can't tell you what it means to me, it's just what I needed, real hot homemade soup, it's been years, I don't think anyone but my mother's ever made me homemade soup, and even she never made mushroom. When you're living alone and traveling a lot you don't get homemade anything."

The forlornness of this last bit makes Gilda glad she didn't touch Nathan's hand. At the same time she's listening for a hint of the patronizing in all this talk of Mom's hot home-made soup, and, when she doesn't hear any, decides Phoebe's pleasure is genuine. Suddenly Phoebe gets up and, standing on tiptoe, peers down into the soup tureen. It's a peculiar gesture. Small as she is, Phoebe could see into the tureen if she just stayed flat on her feet. It's meant to be childlike, meant to charm, but what interests Gilda is that a woman who's gone on commando raids with Sandinista guerrillas would act like an eight-year-old to charm them. "All this soup for us?" Phoebe says.

"I thought I'd make extra in case the students are hungry when they get here," says Gilda and immediately regrets it, hating this image of herself: the homey, solid, faculty wife cooking nourishing soup for the students.

"What students?" Phoebe asks.

"We talked about this in the car," Nathan says. "Some students begged me to let them come by a little later and meet you. I warned them you'd probably be exhausted. But you said it was okay. *Is* it okay? If it isn't, if you're tired or anything, it's fine, I can call and ask them to come some other time—"

"Sure it's okay. I just forgot." Phoebe's voice has taken on such an odd drifty tone that Gilda begins to wonder if she might be suffering slightly from jet lag.

"How long was your trip?" Gilda says.

"Thirty-six hours," says Phoebe. "We got hung up in the Athens airport. Hijack check. The worst part was sitting next to this big fat Palestinian businessman who kept trying to get me to go back and blow him in the airplane bathroom."

There's a silence. Neither Gilda nor Nathan knows quite how to respond. Finally Gilda says, "Yuck," realizing it's a word she's learned from the children. Suddenly she feels the need to bring the children—in spirit—into the room. She knows they've become a kind of talisman for her; when things turn unpleasant or even just socially strained, she runs through their names the way Catholics click off their rosaries.

"You know," Gilda says, "it's a pleasure to cook soup like this for a change. Mostly I don't get a chance. The children wouldn't touch it with a stick."

"How many kids do you have?" Phoebe says, and Gilda's—surprisingly—a little stung that Nathan didn't tell her this in the car. Gilda can't imagine riding for an hour with a stranger and not getting around to that. Though maybe he did, and maybe Phoebe forgot it the way she forgot the students.

"Four," Gilda says. "Sophie's thirteen and Brian's eleven and Ruthie's nine and Danny's seven." Naming them like this makes Gilda acutely aware of how many there are; she feels like Phoebe's a late arrival she's just introduced to a roomful of guests whose names she'll never remember.

"Four?" says Phoebe, and Gilda waits for her to say more. What she's found is that people's responses are so predictable—and so repetitive. In that way having four children is rather like being named Gilda: you get to have the same conversation again and again.

But all Phoebe says is, "That takes courage." This isn't dazzlingly original, either. Lots of people tell Gilda that, but so far none of them have been women who've spent the last ten years careening from war zone to war zone. Gilda almost wants to make Phoebe repeat it for Nathan's benefit since he doesn't seem to be listening, but then Nathan says, "Courage? Stupidity's more like it."

Though Nathan clearly means it as a joke, Gilda's stunned by his betrayal. She knows he doesn't feel that way about her

or himself or the kids. She's so shocked she hears herself bab-
bling things she can't believe she's saying.

"It really wasn't courage," she says. "What happened was,
I became a kind of junkie. I got hooked on being pregnant and
having babies and nursing, and once I got started I couldn't
quit. I'd miss the way newborns smell—their breath and the
tops of their heads have this sweet smell, like candy—and the
next thing I knew I was pregnant again."

Gilda looks over at Nathan, who's smiling slightly and
nodding. He knows what she means, and she feels that this
shared knowledge shames him a little for what he's just said.
When Gilda was pregnant, he couldn't get enough of her—
of touching her, of taking her picture. The sad thing is that
now, when she looks at his book, she skips over those photos
too. Nathan also knows that what Gilda's said is only three-
quarters true. Danny was really an accident. By then they'd
decided to stop having kids, not because they wanted to, but
because they'd gotten superstitious. They'd been so lucky with
the first three; they were frightened of pushing their luck. In
fact, Danny turned out okay, but Gilda's afraid he inherited
all the terrors of that pregnancy; although he's begun to out-
grow it, he's been, at one time or another, scared of nearly
everything. Once, late at night in bed, Nathan referred to
Danny as the runt of the litter and Gilda was horrified at first,
then laughed, because his speaking her own worst fear out
loud made her feel very close to him; it's something only the
other parent can get away with.

Nathan says, "Gilda was the most beautiful pregnant
woman you could imagine," and it occurs to Gilda that
Phoebe—that anyone who knows Nathan's work—knows

exactly how she looked pregnant. Though Gilda's aware that they're very consciously not talking shop here, she's hoping that Phoebe will mention those pictures. But what Phoebe says is, "If you can't cook the children mushroom soup, what can you cook them?"

"Pizza," says Nathan. "Endless pizza."

"What's your favorite meal?" Phoebe asks Gilda, who's so surprised that Phoebe would be interested that the only answer she can come up with is, "Linguine and steamed mussels with hot pepper flakes and garlic and parsley." It's true, she realizes, but if she'd thought a moment longer, she wouldn't have been able to decide.

"That sounds wonderful," says Phoebe. "Maybe you can make it for me sometime."

"And yours?" Gilda says. "Your favorite?"

Phoebe thinks for a while. "Airplane food," she says at last, and her voice goes so vague and drifty again, it's as if she's flying away from them even as they sit there. Gilda's afraid they've bored her with all this talk of children, and knows the time has come to ask about Phoebe's courage—her career, her work. But what's stopping her is this: if people repeat themselves so on the subject of Gilda's name and four children, how much more repetitious must be the questions Phoebe hears all the time. Gilda longs to frame her question in a way no one's happened on yet, but so much dead air's flowing by that eventually she panics and says, "Have you ever been hit?"

Phoebe looks at her strangely. "Only by my lovers," she says. Gilda wonders if this is all Phoebe intends to say on the subject, and has the odd sensation that Phoebe's saving her war stories for a larger and more satisfying audience. But then Phoebe says, "I'll tell you a funny thing. Sometimes out in the field I get this feeling I'm invisible. That no one sees me, that I don't exist. A bullet, a rocket—a bomb couldn't find me. And in a way, I guess, I've learned to make myself invisible. It's like I'm not there—it's how I get all my best shots."

"What a great trick to know," says Gilda. "How do you do it?"

"It's hard to explain," Phoebe says. "But I know when I started feeling that way: as a kid growing up in New York. I used to have to walk home from school along the Bowery, and the bums would all say these dirty things to me. I was *terrified.* So I'd practice making myself disappear so the bums wouldn't see me—and that's how I learned how to do it."

Gilda loves this story, this tale of childhood terror mined for power in later life. She hopes—and is embarrassed for reducing everything to this level again, but there it is—that something similar may work for Danny. She glances over at Nathan, who's got the strangest look on his face. It's hardly enchantment—that much seems clear. But that's all Gilda knows. All those years of practice reading Nathan's mind, and she hasn't a clue to what's on it.

Just then the doorbell rings. "That'll be the students," says Nathan.

"We'll have dessert later," Gilda says, and jumps up from the table.

With each passing year Gilda finds herself avoiding Nathan's students more determinedly. Mostly she's disturbed that they stay the same age while she keeps getting older, but there's also their dogged insistence on calling her Mrs. Wilson no matter how often she asks them to call her Gilda. It makes her feel like Dennis the Menace's neighbor, or like the headmaster's wife in some British public-school novel. One thing she knows is that she doesn't want them calling her Mrs. Wilson in front of Phoebe, so she busies herself clearing dishes while Nathan introduces Phoebe to the students—six of them, Gilda counts, three boys, three girls, though their nearly identical short punky haircuts and designer paratrooper clothes make this difficult to say for sure. It strikes Gilda as ironic that they are the ones dressed like Green Berets while Phoebe, who's probably actually jumped out of airplanes, is wearing silk and those tiny high heels. Making extra trips so as to have something involving to do, Gilda imagines that she's the downstairs maid, and might as well be for all the attention anyone pays her until she shoos them into the living room, urging them to talk and relax while she makes coffee and whips the cream for dessert.

The noise of the electric beater is wonderfully soothing. It blots out everything else as Gilda concentrates on the small miracle of white liquid turning into white solid. She watches the coffee brew, drip by drip, and when she turns away from the counter, she's touched to find Nathan leaning against the doorway between the kitchen and living room, as if he's reluctant to leave her alone in there, working. Hearing Phoebe's clear voice ringing from the other room, Gilda goes and stands beside Nathan to look at what he's watching: Phoebe on the sofa with all the students seated in a circle on the floor, literally at her feet.

Phoebe's in the middle of a story, and it takes Gilda a while to get the gist of it, to realize that Phoebe's volunteering all this, or else the students have been less circumspect than Gilda and Nathan in grilling her for the details of her paramilitary career.

"I had a lover," Phoebe's saying, "a Palestinian commando, trained as a fighter pilot. He'd take me on missions with him so I could take aerial shots of all the bases. Most of them I sold to *Newsweek*. When things calmed down we'd make love everywhere, even standing up in the airplane bathroom."

"Bathrooms on fighter planes?" Gilda whispers to Nathan, but Nathan puts a finger to her lips and says, "Shhh."

"Then one day," says Phoebe, "we took some Israeli fire. We got hit, we went down. My lover was killed. The next thing I knew, I was in an Israeli medivac unit with sixty-two pieces of shrapnel in my back, one in this really strategic place near the base of my spine."

The students make various appreciative, prayerful noises. Wow. Jesus. God. Holy Christ.

"They told me," Phoebe continues, "that I'd been in a coma for thirty-six hours. But here's what I remember: when I opened my eyes, there was this beautiful Israeli nurse. A redhead. She looked just like Rita Hayworth. She had on this great perfume—it smelled like a newborn baby, like candy. And she was bringing me food—homemade mushroom soup, made with real mushrooms from scratch. I'd never had it before, and oh, it was just what I needed. I got to be a kind of junkie for it; once I got started I couldn't stop. And when I began to feel better, she brought me—without my even asking for it—my favorite food: linguine with steamed mussels, hot pepper flakes, garlic, and parsley."

Gilda and Nathan linger a moment to see if Phoebe realizes

they're watching her from the doorway. But she's focused on the middle distance, completely intent on her story; she doesn't know they're there.

Gilda grabs Nathan's hand and pulls him into the kitchen and lets the door swing shut behind them. Gilda's got chills running down her spine, but before she says anything, she wants to be accurate, to know precisely what kind of chills they are. At first she thinks this is how she might feel if she'd come home to find Phoebe trying on all her clothes. But what's happened, she realizes, is less frightening, eerier and more distant—more like the startled, upset way she felt last summer when she found a bird's nest into which had been woven, unmistakably, swatches of that red plaid shirt of Danny's that had mysteriously disappeared from the line. Mostly what concerns Gilda now is that Phoebe be gone before the children get back. How different from her earlier fantasy: that they'd come home early enough for her to show them off. Now Gilda's afraid that if Phoebe meets them, she'll steal something from them too.

Nathan says, "Do me a favor. Don't offer those kids out there any of that mushroom soup. Then they'll really know something's weird."

Gilda nods, then says, "Did you know about this?"

"She said a couple of strange things on the drive back from the airport," Nathan answers. "But I wasn't sure till she started in on that stuff about making herself invisible so the bums wouldn't see her. That's a famous Dorothea Lange story. The other thing is, Phoebe didn't grow up in New York, she grew up in some Nebraska hick town where if a bum ever walked down Main Street, the sheriff would have escorted him onto the first boxcar out of there."

"Is this just starting?" Gilda says. "Has she always been this way? Could she have done all those things she's done—taken all those great pictures—and have always been this way?"

"I don't know." Nathan shrugs. "What difference does it make?"

Gilda wants to tell him that it does make a difference, that, disturbing as the whole thing is, there's reason for relief and possibly even rejoicing here. For the fact is, Phoebe Morrow isn't anyone to be envied; by no means is her life a model life. In no way is her approach to the world any better than Nathan's. The fact is, there's something wrong with her. Some essential component of self is so desperately missing she keeps trying to patch it with borrowed scraps from other people's lives.

Nathan sighs and says, "It's going to be quite a year." And all at once Gilda realizes how childish she's being. Nathan's right; what difference does any of it make? They're too old for easy and false consolations, for the small, mean pleasures of learning that someone whose achievements you've always admired and envied is homely or cursed with an unhappy private life. If Nathan's afraid he's wasted his life, who cares what Phoebe Morrow's done with hers?

Nathan goes to the window and, turning his back to her, looks out. Gilda can't see what he's seeing, but knows, without having to look, there's a rusted swing set and a tangle of bicycles on the lawn. When Danny gets home, he'll cry for Nathan to pull his bicycle out from the bottom, where it always is, its pedal caught in someone else's spoke, and Nathan will study it awhile, then find a way to unhook it.

And now Gilda wants to tell Nathan something else. Quick, before she forgets. She opens her mouth to speak and her hands move as if she's already speaking. She wants to tell him: there *is* a kind of heroism in everyday life, in facing the daily messes which Gilda would often gladly have turned away from.

She's thinking of how, near the end, her grandfather kept falling. How the trim little body he'd always tended so carefully turned first to fat, then useless weight, and fell and fell, so that for a while she feared her house would always seem like a museum of places Pop went down: the guest room, the bathroom, the tight spot between sink and stove she thought they'd never get him out of. She remembers how gently Nathan would lift Pop and walk with him till he stopped feeling embarrassed and shaken, and of how, watching, seeking some way to comfort herself, she'd think of how children learn to walk, how they fell, too—especially Danny, who was so scared. She'd think of herself and Nathan facing each other and calling, Come to Mama, Come to Papa, to the baby tottering back and forth as its parents move farther and farther and farther apart until one or another of them suddenly steps aside and the child, tricked into it, just keeps going.

CRIMINALS

Sarkisian reaches for a book and drops it, then jumps back as if the book is a bottle shattering at his feet. He edges away from the new fiction section, turns, faces into the library, then does another slow, shuffling turn, reminding Alvar of how once, at the Franklin Park Zoo, he peeked behind a fence and saw a large caribou, sick or maybe crazy, trembling, painfully stepping forward and back.

Sarkisian, in a worn-out black coat, is small and stocky, still handsome, with the glossy, swept-back white hair of a fifties French movie peasant patriarch. Alvar and June, the librarian, look at each other, alarmed. Were it anyone else, Alvar would offer help. But Alvar has lived near Sarkisian for eight years without daring to say one word. Sarkisian is a painter's painter, a man who has outlived his friends—Arshile Gorky, Matta, Duchamp—without achieving their fame. But other painters—Alvar is one—know his work. For thirty years Sarkisian has lived near this small Vermont town, essentially a hermit except for occasional visits from his New York dealer.

Eventually Sarkisian comes to, looking more irritated than anything. He picks up the book he's dropped, slams it on the counter, says nothing when June checks it out. June gazes out the window after him. "This isn't the first time," she says. "He really shouldn't be driving." But now it is Alvar who feels slightly weak in the knees, guilty for not having offered to help, and for even thinking that he has just missed the perfect opportunity to make Sarkisian's acquaintance.

At dinner, Marlise's artichoke has her complete attention. Her delicate, pointed face tilts toward it; she could be reading a magazine. Marlise is Swiss, but has been in this country so long she sounds American. Alvar's stopped thinking of her as European, except when she takes things like artichokes so seriously.

Marlise is an arts administrator; she and Alvar moved here from Boston when she was hired to head the South Jericho Cultural Center. Since then she has invited Sarkisian to every opening and show. He never accepts, and though Marlise respects his work, she calls him a selfish old man. Alvar is instantly sorry for having told her about Sarkisian's faltering in the library. It's the same regret he felt long ago when he told his parents how his favorite babysitter sent him up on the roof with a garbage-can lid to boost the TV reception: he would have given anything to unsay it. Most likely Marlise won't be sympathetic—Alvar wouldn't have mentioned Sarkisian if he had had anything else to report.

Alvar's work isn't going well. In Boston he was a medical illustrator and did large thick-paint abstractions. In Vermont he began doing landscapes—moody, expressionistic. On good days he thinks of Burchfield and Albert Pinkham Ryder; on bad, of the muddy army greens and browns of untalented children's art. When they moved here, Alvar had just turned thirty. He'd given himself five years to put together a show; it is now three years past that.

Alvar blames everything on the condos. Last spring a developer put fifty vacation units in the field across from their house. Alvar's best memories are of buggy June evenings, bright October afternoons: he and Marlise cutting through that field on their way to the woods. When the bulldozers came, they walked the edge of the cut, probing it with their sneakers, as if it were a giant scab that might yet heal over. The buildings went up in no time. Now Alvar stays in the yard or drives into town; he can't look at a tree without thinking how soon it will disappear. He thinks of *National Geographic* stories about ecological disasters—El Niño blowing in off the condos, blighting his whole world. Marlise says: This is America. What did he expect?

Marlise spent last month getting funding for a local woman—a terrible weaver who drives around in a van with I WEAVE vanity plates—to take her loom into fifth-grade classrooms. One night Marlise told Alvar that her only consolation was stealing from the state. She hadn't talked like that in ten years. Back in art school, where they met, she took him across the river to Cambridge to hear a Marxist historian lecture on primitive bandits as prototype revolutionaries. He remembers that cinderblock classroom, how conscious he was of her arm beside his, the happiness that came over him as the craggy charismatic professor assured him that he had been right to love Robin Hood. He'd nearly forgotten all that, but now he is glad he didn't. He feels that this memory prepares him, gives him some way to understand what is happening when, after a long silence, Marlise looks up from her artichoke and says that she has an idea.

This is Marlise's idea: they apply for a grant in Sarkisian's name and keep the money themselves. Just that day, a flier had crossed her desk, announcing a new program to bring established artists to small towns. She'd actually thought of Sarkisian: how his silence and stubbornness impoverished them all. The grant is for eight thousand dollars. They have only to fake Sarkisian's signature and résumé; his work is so famous they won't need slides. All Sarkisian had to do is live where he lives and give two public lectures they can pretend he gave. Plenty of visiting poets can testify that you can appear in South Jericho and have not one person come.

"Sarkisian owes guys like you," she says. "Think of it as your grant, the grant you could get if he'd write you the recommendation he's too mean to write. Think of it as our tax money coming back." But all Alvar can think of is that it really is possible to lose track of who someone has become. Though why should that surprise him? Consider their evenings: after dinner Alvar reads while Marlise watches the VCR. She'll rent anything—teen drive-in horror films, low-budget sixties westerns. The last tape he watched with her was a kind of *Mondo Cane* pseudodocumentary about Bombay transsexuals and snake-blood bars in Japan. The funny thing was, it made him feel stuffy for reading, made him wonder if the books he liked—Proust, Tolstoy, biographies of Bloomsbury types and abstract expressionists—weren't just substitutes for a social life of his own.

"It'll be easy," says Marlise. "Someone in some office somewhere will figure Sarkisian wouldn't apply unless he needs the money. They'll be happy to grant him. There isn't one person in arts administration who doesn't at some point start telling you about the Japanese and their national treasures." As she talks, she is surgically cutting the fuzz from her artichoke heart. "Eight thousand dollars," Marlise says. "Think about fifteen acres."

There are many reasons why Alvar doesn't stop her. He is moved that she would risk so much for him; the condos bother Marlise, but, really, he is the one who talks about land. He begins to think she believes in him in ways he has come to doubt. Also, he is intrigued to find that the angry, disaffected, rebellious streak in her wasn't just something put on to intrigue him. There is a mystery in this, and Alvar's reminded of when their differences excited instead of worried him.

Sarkisian doesn't need the money, the state will only waste it. Alvar wants the land.

Everything happens fast. Marlise comes home the next night and tells him she has already sent the application off. There is a rolling deadline; they'll hear in about three months.

Is Marlise the grant-hustler Lady Macbeth? Or the arts-council William Tell, a leveler driven by some primitive justice deeper than Alvar's simple right and wrong? Alvar is interested. He feels that he and Marlise are partners in crime, keeping secrets—not only from the world, but from each other. Perhaps that is what they are looking for as they stare at each other a moment too long, that split-second catch of attention. The air has a buzz, the tension of early flirtation. As they hang out together, cooking in the kitchen, all sorts of things seem, inexplicably, funny.

They never mention Sarkisian and could almost pretend nothing's happened. But when Alvar doesn't see Sarkisian in the library for a few weeks, he nervously asks June if Sarkisian is all right. June says yes, in fact he seems *better*; he's not having those episodes any more. He and Alvar are just coming in at different times.

In the bookstore, Alvar buys a glossy art postcard, a photo of Bonnie and Clyde. Bonnie is pointing a rifle at Clyde and poking him with one finger. They stand on a roadside, a '38 Chevy behind them. Bonnie's long flared skirt strains over her trim little hips and the visible curve of her belly. In her beret, her stylish T-straps, her dress-top like a kid's long-sleeved polo shirt, she is an incredible fox. Alvar laughs out loud. Half-smiling, half-squinting, focused entirely on Clyde, Bonnie reminds him of Marlise.

.   .   .

Alvar and Marlise fall in love all over again. He is triumphant that she is once again more interested in him than in Japanese snake-blood bars. He's disappointed when the passion doesn't translate back into his work, but is, in general, much happier, and even has moments when he would choose his life over anyone's.

Marlise says nothing when the grant money comes through. She carries out the details of cashing and depositing and lets Alvar find out only when their bank statement takes an eight-thousand-dollar jump. Alvar buys champagne and they celebrate, convinced the money is rightfully theirs. It has nothing to do with art, or moral responsibility, but with the immunity and entitlement of new lovers: the world owes them what it begrudges the unloving and unloved. That they should be married so long and still feel this way seems like yet another crime they are getting away with.

One day when Marlise is at work, Alvar goes up past Gilboa and drives around with a real estate agent named Joelle. Chainsmoking Merits, Joelle tells Alvar she's been married three times and has gotten divorced whenever she tried to quit smoking. When they get out of Joelle's car, the air smells so sweet Alvar wants to buy it. Joelle says the acreage is the real estate equivalent of the old lady who sells you all her Fiestaware for thirty bucks. The land includes a granite quarry and a high meadow completely surrounded by mountains. Alvar puts a binder down, and Joelle says, "Sometimes everything comes together."

Alvar waits for a sunny day to show Marlise the land. The

meadow is a steep climb and as Marlise walks ahead, the light hits a red in her hair that Alvar had forgotten. At the top they turn to look at the view. A hawk glides by. The sun is hot. They're sweating. When Alvar kisses the top of her head, Marlise says, "We could be one of those jeans ads in the *Sunday Times Magazine.*" Alvar knows that feeling this young is a trick, and so is thinking that fifteen acres is any protection at all. One TV tower could ruin everything. But right now he feels reprieved, as if time has slowed down for him; if he hurries, there may be enough of it for him to do serious work.

Mornings, Alvar takes pencils, sketch pads, and watercolors and drives up to his land. He fears being corny, like some bereted fruitcake out of the Barbizon School. But drawing takes him beyond self-consciousness, straight back to child-hood Saturdays, to drawing along with the *Jon Nagy Show* and the actual buzz that came up through his arm when he copied something right. He starts with close-ups, Dürer-like botanical drawings, goes on to render the mountains in planes that suggest Cezanne's. The summer sun beating down on his head is part of it. Alvar feels all art history streaming across his sketchbook, until he envisions a way to combine what he's learned about nature with what he knows about paint.

Alvar longs to start painting again, but hesitates; even delay has its pleasures. His worries balance against his curiosity and desire. Finally, he goes back to his studio.

At first there is only pleasure: the smells, mixing colors, the oily gleam of the paint. At first he is entertaining himself, but after a while the choices of color are so right he feels as if something is choosing. The paint does exactly what he wants. He has the same odd tingle up his arm he gets drawing in the fields. His studio even smells like the fields—they've followed him inside. Hours slide away. Working is like a dream from which he wakes thinking: Joelle was right. Everything comes together. El Niño, the condos, stopping smoking—anything can upset the ecosystem. The secret is what will restore it. For a moment, Alvar sincerely believes—or, in any case, remembers a time when he did sincerely believe—that art provides that secret. All the connections—the money, the land, Sarkisian, Marlise, his work—seem complex and mysterious, and make Alvar feel larger than himself, included in a brotherhood embracing Gorky, Sarkisian, Alvar, Michelangelo and his least-gifted apprentice . . .

The better Alvar's work goes, the more he thinks this way—and the more he can't stop wanting to thank Sarkisian in person.

If Alvar told Marlise, she'd say: Thank me. Sarkisian did nothing. Why thank him? She'd say Alvar's wish to contact Sarkisian is a suicide wish to get caught. Alvar too is suspicious: all those stories of perfect crimes spoiled by the murderer's sentimentality, Bonnie and Clyde thinking they could hang out with C.W. and his kindly old dad. Alvar's mystified by this urge which comes over him whenever he stops working. Marlise would point out that a social call is no way to thank a hermit. Still, Alvar imagines some journey or pilgrimage, some risk he must take to thank Sarkisian for being eighty and still painting. Several times he has gotten as far as looking up the number.

One morning Alvar puts down his paintbrush and picks up

the phone and dials. When Sarkisian answers, Alvar explains that he is a painter, lives nearby, has always admired Sarkisian's work. Sarkisian says, "I'm not interested," and hangs up. Alvar is so humiliated he wants to take a nap. He keeps stopping what he's doing to look at himself in the mirror. But that night, when Marlise asks what's wrong, he says, "Nothing." Not telling her reminds him of how he almost didn't mention Sarkisian's stumbling in the library. Now, of course, he's glad he did. Clearly this is different—this time he knows not to tell. But what is familiar is how the impulse towards concealment distances him from Marlise.

Now everything drives Alvar back to work. He rarely visits his land, or the library. Now he paints in the evening too. Marlise has lots of new tapes to catch up on. Alvar finishes one canvas, and though it is nowhere near what he had in mind, immediately starts another.

One day Alvar paints a line that reminds him of Arshile Gorky, and suddenly he knows what he must do. He writes a note saying he has just bought an early painting of Gorky's, a previously unknown masterpiece about which there is some question of authenticity. He wants Sarkisian to see it. He squeezes all this onto the Bonnie and Clyde postcard, and without letting himself reconsider, sends it off.

After a week Alvar gets a reply, a postcard of an empty restaurant dining room: Joe's Steak Out, Jefferson, Mo. On the other side, in a spidery handwriting, "Call me" is written over Sarkisian's phone number and name. This time, when Alvar introduces himself, Sarkisian laughs, a rumbling and wholly unspontaneous Santa Claus "Ho ho ho." "That's some picture!" Sarkisian says. "That Bonnie was one terrific chick! Come to my house next Friday at two. Bring the Gorky, okay?"

Alvar's armpits are wet as he goes into his studio and takes his canvas down from the easel and puts up a clean one. He feels like a character on one of those TV sitcoms based on fakery, more fakery, exposure, confession, reconciliation. What if the prince finds out that My Little Margie isn't royalty? There is never any option but to take deception to its absurd extreme.

In the library, Alvar is afraid that Sarkisian will come in and find him taking out the Gorky book. He forces himself to ask how Sarkisian is. "Pretty chipper," says June. Alvar would have preferred semi-chipper—chipper enough to say something significant, not chipper enough to tell a master-piece from a fake, a forty-year-old painting from one that is barely dry.

The book reminds Alvar of what he'd forgotten: that Gorky spent most of his life imitating other artists. "Then I was with Picasso," Gorky would say. "Now I am with Kandinsky." Alvar loves the irony—imitating the imitator; he sees it as confirmation. What's disappointing is that the Gorky he wanted to do was one of the mysterious, rhapsodic canvases of the artist's late career. The reason he said "early painting" on the postcard was that he thought Sarkisian would be interested in something from the years when he and Gorky lived near each other on Fourteenth Street and were close friends. On the radio in Alvar's studio, the DJ is saying that nothing has felt quite right since Benny Goodman died. Now, hearing the first notes of "Sing Sing Sing," Alvar decides to pile tribute upon tribute and paint a Gorky imitation of Picasso's *The Three Musicians.*

Alvar finds his Picasso book and begins mixing colors, seeking those jazzy oranges and browns. The idea taking shape in his mind is to do a late early Gorky, to create, in fact, the watershed painting marking Gorky's emergence from imitation into genius. Secretly he is hoping to be *with* Gorky, or with Picasso, or even with Benny Goodman, that something of their spirits will rub off on him, guide his hand—just keep him company while he works.

But nothing like that occurs. Gorky isn't there, Picasso isn't there, Alvar's Benny Goodman record sticks and repeats the same maddening phrase. Alvar is utterly on his own. He can't even lose *himself.* He is conscious of everything quotidian and small—passing time, his tongue in his mouth, the laundry he's promised to do. He worries about Marlise, about Sarkisian, about stopping his own work for this—though, in a way, it's more satisfying: the result is so much closer to the intention. Halfway through, Alvar starts seeing the Gorky he had in mind. And yet it gives him no joy. Its satisfactions are all minor, mostly technical, matters of problem-solving, corner-cutting, a little like the pleasure of finding a way to combine two unrewarding errands. Alvar hasn't a prayer that Sarkisian will be fooled.

Now he *should* tell Marlise, for there is always the chance that one discovery will lead to the next—to Marlise getting caught for that grant. Then Alvar will be responsible. But *Marlise* is responsible; it was all her idea in the first place. Even if his meeting with Sarkisian goes well and nothing else comes of it, still, he may never be able to tell Marlise. Though Alvar and Marlise have never mentioned it, they treasured being able to tell each other everything. Suddenly their previous life together, even the worst of it, seems to Alvar as innocent and far away as childhood, and no more possible to recapture. He cannot bring himself to tell Marlise that he has painted a counterfeit Gorky. He hides it when she comes home.

The corn is in tassel and smells of urea—cloying and sweet. Why has Alvar never noticed that the smell of the cornfields is the smell of the nursing home? The land he drives past on his way to Sarkisian's reproaches him. It is early August. He has not been to *his* land for a month. Though he knows better, he can't help feeling the land isn't his any more, that he has lost it. What has he done with his summer? Getting the grant and buying the land seems like ages ago; he remembers irises blooming outside Joelle's office. For comfort, he thinks of the painting he stopped working on in the middle; he can go back to it tomorrow. The thought of it should cheer him, but it doesn't. Last night he watched *Panic in Needle Park* with Marlise; they couldn't look at each other when the junkie couple fought. Alvar thought: Better addicted to heroin than to a VCR. When one of the characters died, Marlise said, "Everyone dies." Her voice had a kind of sob in it which sounded, to Alvar, phony and Garboesque.

The Gorky is in the back of Alvar's pickup. This morning, wrapping it in butcher paper, he'd felt like an Egyptian embalmer. Now he can't stop thinking about Gorky's death. He remembers a conversation from years ago, his art-school friends arguing about Gorky's suicide, each one insisting it happened in a different place. The most success-oriented of them claimed Gorky hanged himself in his gallery; the purist said no, in his studio. The nature painter said outside, from a tree. How romantic his death seemed, especially when they ignored its circumstances—the fire in Gorky's studio, the car wreck, a cancer operation, divorce.

Alvar parks by Sarkisian's mailbox and walks down toward the house. First he sees the metal roof, rusted a rich burnt sienna, then the dark wood siding, weathered to a patina which looks polyurethaned and reminds Alvar of Japanese temples where the whole esthetic is the effect of time. He considers turning around. If he gets no further, it will have been worth it.

Sarkisian greets him at the door. He looks up at Alvar and says, "A Viking!" Alvar cannot pretend he has never seen Sarkisian. He hears himself mumble, "I think we may have met. At the library."

"This library?" Sarkisian studies Alvar more closely. "This country is full of Vikings," he says. "After a while I quit looking." Then Sarkisian laughs, a loud, theatrical poke in the ribs telling Alvar not to take seriously this being lumped with the faceless American Vikings. Alvar is surprised that a hermit would bother maintaining the social skills to be, simultaneously, a charmer and a son of a bitch. "Come in," Sarkisian says.

The main room is just large enough for a table and two chairs, a large cast-iron cookstove, and a kind of daybed covered in red velvet. Every beam is worn to a glossy, exquisite grain; what daylight gets through the one dusty window reminds Alvar of pictures of Central Asia—those smoky blue yurt interiors where children in embroidered beanies play in the shafts of light. But here it's Sarkisian who is dramatically lit as he motions for Alvar to sit down, and takes the chair where the sun finds the white in his hair, the gold of his skin, the hollows of his great cheekbones. Alvar wonders if Sarkisian invited him to come at the hour when he knew the light would do just that. On the table between them is a book, a plastic-covered library copy of The Lives of a Cell. Alvar has never read it, but wants to now; he makes a mental note to check it out.

Sarkisian says, "You are a reader! I can tell! It's how they look at books, sideways, like at a girl. You know that Doisneau photograph, that very bourgeois French gentleman window-shopping with his wife, his eyes are over here, there is a painting of a naked woman? That is how readers look at books. I am a painter, but literature is my love. I went to my friends' studios, but first, before I saw their work, first I looked at their books."

Alvar says, "I read all the time." His voice is strained and unrecognizable. He hasn't sounded like this since he and Marlise fell in love. That they were so scared of each other made him realize how serious it was. Now he thinks: I am thirty-five years old, and I sound like an art-school girl on a date.

"All right!" says Sarkisian. "Here is a question. Who was the greatest writer who ever lived?"

How can Alvar answer? "I give up," he says. "Proust?"
"That homo?" says Sarkisian. "That social climber? Let me
tell you: Henry James."

Alvar says, "Henry James?"

"Proust is like stuffing your face with a cream puff,"
Sarkisian says. "Some complicated French dessert. Henry
James is clean—like good strong caviar. Proust is a skating
bug, skating ever-bigger circles on the surface of the pond.
Henry James is a diver. He goes deep." Sarkisian plunks his
fist on the book and leans across the table toward Alvar.
"Deeper and deeper," Sarkisian tells him. "That is the pur-
pose of art."

Alvar things: Fish eggs? Henry James? Is Sarkisian out of
his mind? Still, this "deeper and deeper" thrills him. He feels
that he has gotten advice here, great advice about art. Deeper
and deeper is something to point his life toward. He also
suspects it's the kind of advice that is good for about twenty
minutes. Deeper and deeper could be the punch line in one
of those holy-man life-is-a-fountain shaggy-dog jokes.

"We will have time," Sarkisian says. "We will talk about
Henry James."

Alvar can't believe he is hearing this. Does Sarkisian mean,
time today, or in the future? Maybe they can be friends. Alvar
imagines painting till late afternoon on those suicide-gray
winter days, then driving to Sarkisian's. Perhaps, in time, he
can even tell Sarkisian about the grant they collected in his
name, and they will laugh at how life imitates Henry James:
Alvar and Marlise, one of those Jamesian adventurer couples.
He will take Sarkisian to the land, show him what they have,
in a way, bought together.

"Do me a favor," Sarkisian says. "You are a literary man. See that poem up there on the door? Maybe you can tell me who wrote it. I don't know."

The door he is pointing at is open. To read the card tacked up to it, Alvar has to step into a small adjoining room, empty except for an armchair in the middle. On all four walls and the ceiling are pasted up movie-star photos, art reproductions, newspaper clippings, most of them yellowed with age and shellac, though some are newer. The newest, Alvar's flattered to see, is his postcard of Bonnie and Clyde. He wants to go over and look at Bonnie's foxy familiar smile. But he's afraid to, afraid of Sarkisian, and of the room making him feel like a button in some Victorian housewife's decoupage box. "My study," Sarkisian says.

Alvar reads the poem, copied out by hand. "As I was going up the stairs / I met a man who wasn't there. / He wasn't on the stairs today. / I hope to God he stays away." Alvar can't help saying, "This?"

"That," says Sarkisian. "Who wrote it? Any ideas?"

"I don't know," Alvar says. "Ogden Nash?"

"Very good!" says Sarkisian. "I doubt it."

They both fall silent. A few moments later Sarkisian says, "Here's what I can't understand. All those fellows in Henry James going through life without sex. Young people should be in love all the time. Like Clyde and Bonnie. When I was young, I fell in love every day. Then—if they want to be artists—then they have to give all that up."

"Give it up why?" Alvar asks, smiling lamely.

"Too distracting," says Sarkisian.

Alvar wants to say: What about Picasso? He wants to say:

No one believes this anymore. Nobody insists that artists starve and live like hermits and go crazy and kill themselves. New York is full of artists—real artists—eating in first-class restaurants. Even Gorky had a wife—two wives. Two daughters. Then Alvar thinks of how they had left him by the end, and of Gorky's suicide note: "Goodbye my loveds." Maybe Sarkisian is right. So that when Sarkisian asks, "Are you married?" Alvar is astonished to hear himself say, "No."

So: yet another thing Alvar wishes he could unsay. He feels that he has betrayed Marlise, that ten years of loving and being faithful to her count for nothing. Waves of guilt and sadness roll over him, even as a meaner thought crosses his mind: What if he and Sarkisian do become friends? How will he explain Marlise? He considers how all this began and will end in deception. Alvar is a counterfeiter, Sarkisian an incredible ham. Nothing will ever come of this but lies and more lies. How foolish he was to hope for anything more. But even so, when Sarkisian says, "Now the Gorky, you have brought it?" Alvar thinks: Not yet.

Because the painting will end everything. Sarkisian will spot the counterfeit, and Alvar will have to leave. And though Alvar knows he was wrong to expect more, still some part of him goes on hoping—though for what he doesn't know. It reminds him of how, just before he and Marlise became lovers, they would linger in each other's presence, with nothing more to say but reluctant to part, and even a little angry.

Alvar excuses himself and goes to get the painting from the truck; he almost drives off. Back inside, he unwraps the canvas. Sarkisian examines it a moment, then says, "Where did you get this?" Alvar pauses. There is still time to confess, to accept his humiliation and get out. He says, "London," where he has never been. "At an auction."

Finally Sarkisian says, "I remember when Gorky painted this."

Alvar is conscious of steam escaping quietly from a kettle on the stove, and that he is holding his breath as Sarkisian says, "I will tell you something about Gorky. None of us thought he could paint. Personality, yes. But talent? Talent, no. The joke was: Gorky will be an old man and still imitating Kandinsky. Then one day I ran into him on Fourteenth Street, he dragged me up to his studio. I saw there this painting. This one here. I thought: Another imitation Picasso. But then I saw that it was different, not just Picasso—but Gorky. Understand?"

"Yes," Alvar says, suppressing a crazy desire to laugh. He has gotten away with it! He knows it is nothing to be proud of. But maybe Gorky's spirit was working through him. And really, what harm does it do for Sarkisian to recover these memories, this moment of connection with his old friend?

"I told Gorky we must celebrate," Sarkisian goes on. "Between us we had a dollar. Gorky said, 'Let's go to Central Park and rent a boat.' It was a beautiful day. So we went to the park and went out on the lake and rowed a while, and pretty soon we saw two girls on the shore. Beautiful girls! We said, 'Come for a ride!' The girls got in the boat. We rowed out again, talking, very polite. Suddenly Gorky began rowing like mad, leaning way back. I said, 'Gorky, what the hell are you doing?' Then Gorky winked at me and I saw: each time he leaned back, he was looking up those girls' dresses!"

Sarkisian laughs, as does Alvar. Alvar feels privileged to
have heard this, feels that he has been taken back in time
to the day when a great painter's work turned a corner. He
remembers that sense he had—when he first bought the land
and started painting again—of a brotherhood, a line of artists
spanning past and future. So what if the painting isn't a
Gorky? Meeting Sarkisian was a blessing, even if the agents
of that blessing were petty crimes. Alvar thinks: Deeper and
deeper. He promises himself to remember Gorky and Sarkisian
in that rowboat, to keep that image with him, like part of
his own memory, changing his whole future life.

Then Alvar thinks: Change it how? And now, though he
tries, he cannot imagine a different life—happiness and success in his work. He cannot imagine any life but more of the
one he is living. Slowly the largeness of Alvar's moment
leeches away to nothing and Alvar knows beyond any doubt
that he isn't Gorky, he isn't even Sarkisian. The promise of
Gorky's life—that genius can reveal itself at any minute—won't
necessarily hold for Alvar's. For one thing, he is a smaller person. He should have begged to see Sarkisian's work. But all
Alvar wanted was for Sarkisian to like him. Even now, he is
reacting in a small way, sizing himself against Sarkisian and
Gorky. Alvar will always be the slow learner, the acolyte, the kid
you send up to the roof with a garbage-can lid. Now he says, "I
know a story about Henry James."

"What's that?" asks Sarkisian.

"I used to live in Cambridge," Alvar says, "across from the
Mount Auburn Street Cemetery. One night I brought a girl
home. I pointed out the window. I said, 'That's where Henry

and William James are buried.' And she said, 'Too bad for them.' "

There's a silence. Sarkisian looks at Alvar. Alvar has not told this story for a long time. Now he cannot believe he ever thought it was funny—or that he is telling cemetery stories to an eighty-year-old man. But what shocks him most is how, in the years since he last told it, he has crossed over a line. He is now on Sarkisian's side.

Maybe the reason he told it is that the girl in the story was Marlise. He has brought Marlise's voice in here; they have heard what she has to say. Alvar knows exactly when she said that—they had come back from one of those bandit lectures. And now he knows why he told it. Because Marlise was right: death is the bandit, the leveler putting everyone in the same line. The young men rowing on the lake, looking up girls' dresses; the caribou, wacked-out and trembly, shuffling back and forth in the Franklin Park Zoo; Gorky, Sarkisian, Alvar—they each have a place in that line. Its length is what Bonnie is measuring as she points her arm and her rifle at Clyde; it's the secret of her foxy smile. Because if *that* is her measure, the only distance that counts, then right now, right for the present, she and Clyde are lucky.

THE BANDIT
Was My
NEIGHBOR

.

Un warm summer evenings
my grandmother sits on the traffic island in the middle of
Sixth Avenue and tells Mrs. Russo about her bandit lover.

Buses speed past, blowing fumes in their faces. Drunks lurch
toward them, begging for quarters. But the two old widows,
roosting on their bench like enormous gray-headed chickens,
never notice. For they are not really on that bench, or on that
grimy concrete strip, or even in New York City.

They are in Sicily, fifty years ago, in the days of Italo Giuliano.

Ordinarily my grandmother is a quiet woman who rarely talks. But when she tells the story of Italo Giuliano, she speaks in the grand style, and her voice is assured and strong.

"In America," she says, always beginning the same way, "whenever I heard people telling stories about the great bandits, I wanted to remind them that Italo Giuliano, the greatest bandit leader of all, was born in my own town. But I was smart. I kept quiet. I thought it would be foolish to let strangers know I once had inside information about a man like Italo Giuliano."

"Not only foolish," agrees Mrs. Russo, "but dangerous! You can never tell when they'll use something like that against you."

"Yet in fact, Mrs. Russo," continues my grandmother, "I had the most inside information of all. Because ever since I was a baby in my cradle, my window looked directly into his.

"Our families were in business together. My father bought sheep from the local herdsmen. Italo's father sold the mutton in his shop. The partnership had been started by our grand-fathers—two best friends, so distrustful of each other that they built their houses a few feet apart, to keep each other honest.

"They spied on one another constantly. Whenever the herdsmen came to our house, Italo's grandfather appeared at his window, pretending to check on the weather. Whenever the Giuliano family ate lunch, my grandfather watched care-fully, making sure that his partner hadn't taken the crown roast for himself.

"But by the time Italo and I were born, our grandfathers

were dead. And our fathers, members of a more enlightened generation, no longer kept up the constant surveillance.

"I was the only one with the spy's blood still running in my veins. And so, all through the rainy days of my childhood, I stood at my window and watched Italo Giuliano.

"It must have been the pure thrill of spying that attracted me, because it wasn't a very interesting sight. All Italo ever did was read. Day after day, I watched him mumbling to himself and turning the pages with a faraway look in his eye. He was oblivious to everything else. He never even flinched when his brothers teased him, pelting him with chunks of raw mutton, or gory sheep's hearts that splashed his books with blood.

"Our village was very isolated, high up in the mountains, fifty kilometers from the nearest school. So Italo had been obliged to teach himself. He began with the words on flour sacks and tobacco packages. He read the family Bible seven times. He borrowed the priest's missal and pored over the senseless Latin. He even took to standing at the crossroads, flagging down passing trucks and badgering the drivers for newspapers from distant cities.

"Whenever Mrs. Giuliano heard about that, there was something to see from my window. 'This reading is turning you into a bandit!' she'd scream at her son.

"Right from the start, Italo was a sensitive boy. After each of his mother's harangues, he'd run away from home, and crawl through the narrow alley between our houses.

" 'Angela,' he'd whisper up at me. 'I'm on the run. Take me in.'

"I'd let him stay in my mother's kitchen until the good

smells made him so hungry that he forgot his quarrel. But one day, even I lost patience. What good is spying, I thought to myself, if you're always spying on the same old thing?

" 'Italo,' I said, 'maybe your mother's right. Why do you waste your time reading? Do you like it when your brothers tease you? Do you want everyone to call you a bookworm?'

" 'Yes,' replied Italo Giuliano, 'I do.'

"I was just a little girl then, with a little girl's mind. But suddenly, as I looked at my friend, I understood as well as any woman: Italo wanted to be teased about his reading. That way, no one would tease him about his looks.

"For Italo Giuliano was the homeliest boy in Sicily. Even as a child, his skin was covered with purple cysts the size of grapes. His nose looked as if God had stuck a lump of dough in the middle of his face. His eyebrows grew together over his nose in one long eyebrow which reminded me of a frowning, hairy mouth.

"When he was small, the village children teased him mercilessly, saying that he resembled the putrefying sheep's heads behind his father's shop. Yet by the time he started to read, they no longer called him 'the Sheep.' Italo thought that he owed his reprieve to his new knowledge, but he was wrong. The children's sudden kindness had nothing to do with his reading. Rather, it was this: everyone in the village had begun to recognize the sweet nature beneath that sour face.

"He was the most generous and patient boy who ever lived," says my grandmother, hugging herself so hard that the flesh trembles on her arms. "He was my best friend, he would have done anything for me. Whenever my father hit me, I ran to Italo. Whenever I was sick, he sat on my bed and read aloud to me. And whenever I woke up screaming from a bad dream, I'd call across the alley, and make Italo walk with me until I was calm."

"Didn't your parents worry?" asks Mrs. Russo. "A little girl like that, staying out all night with her boyfriend?"

"They wished they had reason to worry," says my grandmother. "They would have liked me to marry Italo someday, for business reasons. And they knew how I admired his sweetness. But they also knew that the combination of his good nature and his homely face meant that I would never love him as a man.

"It was that way with all the girls. We loved Italo so much that we let him stay near us even after we'd started chasing the other boys away with stones. 'Look, Italo,' we'd say. 'Look how much we love you.'

"But it wasn't really love. Love was what we felt for those other boys, who teased us so meanly that we had to chase them away. And Italo was the one we punished for their sins.

"We took terrible advantage of him. We asked him for favors, sent him on errands, and never did anything in return. Sometimes, when our mothers gave us custard, Italo would ask us to save him the last bite. 'Of course,' we'd say. But we always forgot."

"Then why did he put up with it?" interrupts Mrs. Russo. "Were you girls his only friends?"

"He was too good-natured to resist," replies my grandmother. "Besides, he had another friend, a boy."

"And who was that?"

Of course, Mrs. Russo knows the answer. She's heard this story a thousand times. But this last question is her favorite;

she's been leading up to it all along. And now, she settles back on the bench, waiting with delight. "What was his name?" she asks.

"His name," says my grandmother, "was Italo Giuliano."

"They were distant cousins," she continues, "related by some long-ago marriage that no one could remember. Yet after my neighbor was christened Italo, the other Mrs. Giuliano, the café owner's wife, stormed through the village, cursing their kinship to high heaven.

" 'All my life,' she said, 'I've wanted a son named Italo. And now that old witch has beaten me to it. But I'll have my way yet. I'll name my next son Italo, even if it means that there will be two boys in this town with the same name.'

" 'Don't do it,' the women advised her. 'You'll doom them to confusion. They'll be hobbled for life.'

" 'Then I'll call him Italo Salvatore,' said the café owner's wife. 'But that's the farthest I'll go.'

"Yet the villagers need never have worried about confusing the two Italos, for no two boys could have been more different. Italo Salvatore grew tall and handsome. His eyes had a dreamy look, like those of the saints on the chapel wall. Unlike my neighbor, he was illiterate, and very charming—with a flashing wink, a quick smile, and a terrible mean streak.

"At first, the two Italos ignored each other. But before they entered their teens, they suddenly decided to become friends. After that, they acted as if their common name was some hilarious private joke. Whenever the handsome boy was called, my neighbor would answer; when a traveling dentist pulled my neighbor's tooth, the other Italo faked a howl of pain. For a while, they even dressed alike and claimed to be twins.

"And so the view from my window began to change. Late at night, Italo still sat alone, reading. But in the evenings, he and his friend played together, pretending to be pirates, soldiers, bandit kings.

"Italo Salvatore was always the leader in those games. It seemed wrong. Not only was my neighbor older, but, even then, he had the courage and ingenuity that were to make him the most beloved bandit chief in all Sicily. But the other's mean streak gave him an advantage. Like the girls, he mistreated his good-natured friend. He bossed him around like an unpaid servant. He even teased him about his looks, saying that no sensible girl would ever love a boy whose eyebrows grew together over his nose.

"Italo Salvatore had no such problems, and that, too, was a source of power. For all the village girls adored him, adored that dreamy expression. Naturally they threw stones at him. But after they'd chased him away, they surrounded my neighbor and pumped him for information about his handsome friend.

" 'Listen,' they'd say, 'what does that stupid Italo Salvatore say about us, behind our backs?'

" 'He never mentions you,' beamed Italo, proud to be the chosen confidant of so many beautiful girls.

"And so the two boys complemented each other. Their friendship seemed to increase the homely one's familiarity, and the handsome one's mystery."

.   .   .

"Eventually Italo Salvatore also became my friend. At first he didn't like me, and my neighbor kept us apart, as if he were unwilling to share us. But gradually, Italo Salvatore learned that I was clever, that he could treat me like another boy; and my neighbor came around. So the three of us began to play together.

"Every Saturday morning, we went for long walks through the fields. My neighbor and I always lagged slightly behind, while Italo Salvatore ran ahead, searching for buried treasure. Sometimes he'd find an old spoon, a rusty coin, a used-up cartridge. Once he unearthed a small tortoiseshell comb and gave it to me, saying that girls' things made him sick.

"At home, I washed the comb, and wrapped it in a cloth, as if it really was a treasure. For in giving me that present, Italo Salvatore had won my heart. Not that I adored him, like those giggling girls. But I didn't want him to treat me like another boy.

"And so, on those Saturday morning walks, all my clever remarks were aimed at Italo Salvatore. I wanted to impress him, to intrigue him, to make him laugh. I even bought a miniature of St. Michael, because the saint's dreamy expression reminded me of Italo Salvatore.

"Sometimes I wondered if my neighbor was hurt by my crush on his handsome friend. But Italo never seemed to mind; he never seemed to notice. His sweet good nature never changed.

"Of course he doesn't care, I thought, he doesn't think of me that way.

"In fact, he didn't seem to think of anyone that way. For, in those troublesome times, Italo alone seemed unaffected by

those strange things that were happening to the rest of us,
those changes, those daily surprises. He grew taller; his voice
deepened; his complexion got worse. Yet he never seemed
confused, unhappy, full of new secrets.

"Lucky Italo, I thought. It's easy for him.

"But late one night, as I stood at my window, I saw something that made me realize I'd been wrong.

"It was a hot evening in July. Italo's family had gone out to
escape the heat, leaving him alone. Spying from my darkened
room, I saw him take the pincers which his mother used on
stubborn pinfeathers. I saw him stare into the mirror, tense
with concentration.

"And then I saw Italo Giuliano tweeze the hairs from that
place where his eyebrows grew together, above his nose."

"So perhaps Italo's change was just slow in coming. For by the
next summer, when Italo Salvatore returned from that fateful
trip to Palermo, my neighbor was clearly ready to change something deeper than his overgrown eyebrows.

"The boys were fifteen. Early in June, Italo Salvatore had
gone with his father to see an uncle in the city. And he came
back a different man. The city had turned him into a gangster.
He'd bought a sheepskin jacket, which he wore with the collar
turned up. He chain-smoked cigarettes. He mumbled out of
the corner of his mouth. And he narrowed his eyes into such
thin slits that I could no longer see their dreamy expression.

"Immediately my neighbor began to copy him. From my
window, I saw him stretching the collar of his sweater until it
hung in rolls around his neck. And as he narrowed his eyes and

twisted his mouth, he looked so exceptionally homely that I almost cried.

"Within a week, the two Italos became the village bullies. They shook down children for pennies. They insulted the girls with dirty names. 'Stay away from those two,' our mothers warned us. 'They're nothing but trouble.'

"If that had been true, we would never have listened to our mothers; we would have worshipped those boys like Jesus. But we knew they were only imitation gangsters, pretending to be tough; and we despised them for it. Italo Salvatore lost all his fascination for me. And my neighbor turned so nasty that I couldn't stand to see him. We stopped speaking, and I mourned the loss of Italo's good nature as if it were a dead man.

"All the village girls felt as I did—all, that is, but one. For is was rumored that little Maria Gozzi had become Italo Salvatore's mistress, and was meeting him at night, behind the church.

"My neighbor, on the other hand, had given up his love. He would have died before he read another book. Mrs. Giuliano had gotten her wish, but it brought no peace to the family. As I spied on them from my window, I saw her raging harder than ever, cursing Italo's rotten gangster ways.

"One night, after one of those battles, a strange thing happened. Italo stormed out of his house, and squeezed through the narrow alley, just as he'd done as a boy.

" 'Angela,' he whispered, 'I'm on the run. Take me in.'

" 'No,' I said. 'You've gotten too nasty. Be a gangster if you want, but not in my house.'

"But a moment later, I changed my mind. For the sake of

our old friendship, I let him in; for the sake of those nights he'd comforted me, I let him sit on my bed. But that evening, he couldn't sit still. Suddenly, he sprang toward me, pinning me against the pillows.

" 'Angela!' he cried. 'All week Italo Salvatore's been telling me what it's like to kiss Maria Gozzi, and I want to try it myself. Please, let me do it with you, as an experiment, just to see what it's like!'

" 'You're crazy!' I screamed. 'That's no way to ask a girl. And even if it was, I wouldn't do it with you.'

" 'That's just what Italo Salvatore told me,' said my neighbor. 'All the girls protest like that.' So he refused to believe me, and kept on pressing his homely face against mine until he saw I was serious. Then, without a word, he got up and left the house.

"The next morning, as I looked across the alley, I noticed that Italo's bed was empty. And it stayed empty, for two years."

My grandmother sighs and reaches down to brush some imaginary dust off her thick black stockings. "A lot happens in two years," she says. "Maria Gozzi got pregnant. Italo Salvatore got married. He settled down, took over the management of his father's café, and soon developed such a paunch that I wondered what I ever saw in him.

"I, too, settled down. That fall, my parents began mentioning Anthony Bruno, ten times a day. 'He's a good boy,' said my mother. 'He'll inherit his father's bakery. He'll take good care of you.'

"I took the hint; it was time for me to marry, anyway. So Anthony and I moved into my father's house. He worked in the bakery all day; at night he sat in the café playing cards with his friends. It was comfortable, married life. It was the way everyone lived.

"I was five months pregnant with my first child when Italo Giuliano came home.

"By then, I'd stopped spying on the Giuliano family. So it was only an accident that I first saw Italo from the window. I stood very quietly, and stared. I saw that he'd kept his gangster ways. He'd bought a real sheepskin jacket, heavy boots, and a funny cap, like a shepherd's. I noticed that he'd grown a little less homely. And later that evening, when he came to visit, I looked closer, and saw something else: I saw that he'd brought his old good nature home with him.

"At first, I was a little nervous when he kissed me hello, for I remembered that night when he'd pressed his face against mine. I pushed my belly forward, wishing that I showed more than I did. But, as I watched him greeting my family in his calm, friendly way, I knew I had nothing to fear. Indeed, he was so much the trusted old friend that my husband Anthony didn't hesitate to go play cards, leaving us alone.

"After Anthony left, we couldn't talk. There was a distance between us, even wider than that angry space which had come between us at the start of Italo's gangster days. Once again, at least, we were pleasant to each other. But we were no longer friends.

" 'Where have you been?' I asked him.

" 'In Palermo,' he said.

" 'What's it like?' I said.

"He began to tell me about Palermo. But it sounded wrong, like a description he'd read in a book, or had heard from Italo Salvatore. He wasn't describing any place he'd ever been.

" 'All right,' I interrupted. 'All right. What do you do there?'

" 'I do what I want,' he said. 'And no one takes advantage of me.' Then he kissed me goodbye and went home.

"That night, as I lay beside my husband Anthony and stared into the darkened windows of the Giuliano house, I tried to be happy. 'It's good,' I told myself. 'Italo's come back.' But suddenly, I recalled that distance between us and felt the loss of my childhood, felt it like an empty space, like a missing tooth.

"As it happened, the other villagers were even more upset by Italo's return. They began to whisper about him, spreading rumors so ugly that mothers sent their children out to play before they would even discuss it. It was disgusting, they said. Italo Giuliano had seduced a fourteen-year-old girl, Italo Salvatore's little sister. He had bewitched her, filled her head with funny ideas. He'd taken her home with him, and was living shamelessly, in sin, beneath his poor mother's own roof.

"By the time I heard the rumors, I knew they were true. For I had seen it from my window. Night after night, I watched them making love, their bodies glistening in the moonlight. I watched Italo whispering in her ear, telling her stories of city life, of Palermo, of God knows what.

"It was just the kind of thing I'd hoped to see when, as a girl, I'd spied on Italo. But it didn't make me happy; I wanted it to end.

"Of course, it couldn't last. The whispers were growing louder. The scandal could no longer be contained. Three times a day, Mrs. Giuliano went to mass, begging the Virgin to end her shame.

"Then one night, as if in answer to her prayers, a band of men converged on the Giuliano house. Led by Italo Salvatore, they seized the sleeping couple and dragged them out of bed. Beating and kicking them, they took them to the edge of town, and threatened to kill them if they ever returned.

"But three weeks later, when the girl came back, she was such a pitiful sight that even the cruelest of them couldn't bring himself to execute that harsh sentence.

"I still remember how she stood there, wailing, wringing her sunburned hands. 'Kill me!' she cried. 'Go ahead and kill me! But I can't live like that!'

"And it was then that we learned the truth about Italo Giuliano. That imitation gangster, that homely bookworm, that good-natured boy—he had become a notorious bandit! He was a fierce, clever criminal, famous for his bravery. He roamed all through Italy with a band of men who ate raw meat and picked at their body lice with stilettos. Already he'd robbed ten banks, a dozen trucks, fifty mail shipments, and a hundred landowners.

" 'He's been doing it for two years!' said the girl. 'Ever since he left this place the first time. Everyone in Sicily's heard of it, everywhere but here, in this know-nothing town, where no one's ever heard of anything!'

"Italo's mother shrieked and fainted. I helped her to her feet, and took her home.

" 'Get me my mourning dress,' she moaned. 'I'll grieve for my son as if he were dead.'

" 'Don't be silly,' I told her. 'Now everyone in town will worship him like Jesus. And now he'll never die.'

"I was right. From then on, the townspeople cross-examined every passing stranger for news of Italo Giuliano. Like their hero, ten years before, they stopped cars at the crossroads and pestered their drivers. Until then, the isolated villagers had viewed the outside world only as a source of rare luxuries, like tobacco. But suddenly their bandit son had pushed them into modern life. For them, all history was the legend of Italo Giuliano: He robbed from the rich to feed the poor. He never killed, except in self-defense. He'd emerged unhurt from a thousand ambushes. He was such a beloved leader that men died out of loyalty to him. And though he'd stolen more than two billion lire, he gave it all to charity, and lived as a poor man.

"The villagers began to regret the inhospitable treatment they'd given Italo during his last visit. After all, they said, it wasn't really such a sin for a great hero to have come courting a sweet local girl.

"In private, though, they wondered about the real reason for that visit. It was said that beautiful women were always offering themselves to the bandits. Why, then, did Italo come after a scrawny little thing like the Giuliano girl?

"The dishonored girl became a local celebrity. 'He did it for me,' she proclaimed proudly. 'He came back for love of me.'

"Italo Salvatore did everything possible to steal his sister's glory. 'No,' he'd say. 'He came back because of me. I was his old friend, and he seduced my sister to settle an old debt.'

"But I knew they were both wrong. For I alone knew the

true reason for Italo's visit: he had known that I'd be at my
window, night after night, watching him play with that skinny
girl. And he wanted me to be ready when he returned again."

"And I was ready," says my grandmother, shutting her eyes
for a moment, just as she does when she samples the parsley
at the greengrocer's. "In the meantime, though, five years
passed. Anthony inherited the bakery; we moved into our own
house. And with three children underfoot, I had no time to
dream about bandits. Still, whenever I heard rumors of my old
friend's exploits, I'd feel that strange, empty pain, like a missing
tooth.

"But on the night Italo finally came, I wasn't thinking of
him. I'd put the children to bed. Anthony was off at the café,
praying for three aces. And I was sitting near the window, wondering how I could make a pound of tomatoes last a week.

"Then, suddenly, I heard him. 'Angela,' he whispered. 'I'm
on the run. Take me in.'

"For a moment, as I looked down, I expected to see the old
alley, with the Giuliano house across the way. But all I saw that
night was Italo's face—shining, beautiful in the moonlight.
All those awful cysts were gone, leaving small marks which
made him look rough and handsome, like a wolf. He was sunburned; a pale scar ran across his forehead, down through that
place where his eyebrows had once grown together. But it was
not just his face which had changed. His whole expression
was different. He had the look of a man who has won a
staring contest with his own death.

" 'Italo,' I said. 'What's happened to you?'

" 'Nothing,' he said. 'Can I come in?'

" 'No,' I told him. 'Wait. I'll come out.'

"That night, I followed Italo Giuliano to the meadow."

My grandmother is a modest woman, who would never dream of dwelling on the details of that night. But she sighs and gazes off into the traffic in such a way that tears of envy spring to Mrs. Russo's eyes.

"The next morning," she continues, "I opened my eyes to see a golden bracelet on Italo's arm. Shining discs hung from the bracelet; each was engraved with a single word. 'Honor,' I read, 'Danger. Courage. Resourcefulness. Justice. Fidelity. Homesickness.'

"At last, the bracelet's jangling woke Italo. 'A bandit's life,' he said, pointing to the words on the discs. 'It wakes me every morning.'

"I couldn't look at him. 'Fidelity,' I said. 'Homesickness. What does that mean?'

" 'It means I'll come back to you,' he said.

" 'When?' I said.

" 'At least once before I die.'

" 'But why should I believe you?'

" 'You know me,' he said. 'I never lie.' Then he kissed me, got to his feet, and walked off across the meadow.

"I went home and lied. I told my husband Anthony that my stomach was bad, that I'd been sick all night in the fields. But I knew Italo hadn't lied. So I believed he'd come back, believed him so completely that I didn't even worry when the soldiers came looking for him.

"Although Mussolini had just come to power," says my grandmother, "none of my neighbors had ever heard of him. But once again, Italo Giuliano brought history to our village. One afternoon the army rode into town and ordered us to gather in the marketplace.

" 'Il Duce is your leader now' said the black-shirted captain. 'And he has sworn to protect his people from the vicious mountain bandits who have been oppressing you. We know that Italo Giuliano comes from this district, and we would appreciate your help in hunting him down.'

"The captain was an oily little man, who reminded me of my daughter's painted dolls. When my neighbors sneered at his request, I thought that he was probably well accustomed to such sneers.

" 'Good luck to him,' said the villagers. 'He'll never get one of us to do that traitor's work.'

"But I was afraid that they were wrong. I was afraid that there was one who would.

"A few days later, my husband Anthony went to play cards, and came home with the news that the doors of the café had been boarded shut. Italo Salvatore had left home."

"And what happened then?" asks Mrs. Russo. "Did the two Italos meet? Did that no-good man betray his best friend?"

"Then," says my grandmother, "Anthony and I went to America. The war was reaching up into the mountains. My husband Anthony, always a practical man, knew that things were getting worse, and decided to sell the bakery and take us to some relatives in New York.

"On the night before we left, I went back to my old

house. Looking through the window, I saw Mrs. Giuliano, kneeling before a statue of the Virgin, praying for her son's return.

" 'Don't worry,' I wanted to call to her. 'He'll be back.' And then I remembered: when Italo Giuliano returned to the village, I would no longer be there.

"So Anthony and I came to Carmine Street. Here in America life was so different, I sometimes thought that all my memories had happened to someone else. When I remembered that view from my window, it seemed like something in a dream. And so, ten years ago, when a stranger knocked on my door, I didn't think of Italo Giuliano. When a stranger knocks in America, you think of boys selling magazines; you don't expect bandits from the wilds of Sicily.

"On that day, I opened my door to find a dapper old gentleman, with a bristling red moustache. He was well dressed, in a black coat and a trim gray hat. But his hair was oddly streaked, as if he'd dyed and redyed it many times. His eyes were nervous. He reminded me of a fox.

" 'What can I do for you?' I said.

" 'Let me introduce myself,' he answered.

" 'I haven't got much time,' I told him. But already, he'd opened his fist. In his palm were two gold discs, engraved with the words 'Fidelity' and 'Homesickness.'

" 'Italo Giuliano!' I cried.

" 'I was his first lieutenant,' said the man, fixing me with his fox's eyes.

" 'Come in,' I said. 'Come in. How is Italo?' I asked, as soon as he'd stepped inside. 'What's he doing now? Is he still in the moutains, running with those bandits?'

"The man looked at me, puzzled. 'He's dead,' he said. 'He's been dead forty years.'

" 'No,' I said. 'No.'

" 'Yes,' he said. 'I was there. Would you like me to tell you the story?' Then, without waiting for a reply, he sat down at the kitchen table, and began:

"In the spring of 1933, one of our spies returned to camp with the news that a lone man had been asking around for Italo Giuliano, searching for him everywhere.

" 'What sort of man?' Italo asked.

" 'A fool,' replied the spy. 'And probably an informer. He dresses like a gangster, like a teenage kid pretending to be a gangster. He wears an old leather jacket with the collar turned up. He chain-smokes cigarettes, narrows his eyes, and mumbles out of the corner of his mouth.'

" 'I know the man,' said Italo Giuliano. 'Go bring him back.'

"We thought it odd that Italo should invite a stranger to our camp, at such a crucial and dangerous time. But Italo had never failed us before. He was the best leader who ever lived and we trusted him completely.

"But when the stranger finally arrived, and we saw what kind of man he was, we began to wonder if something had impaired our chief's judgment.

"The stranger was a fool. His gangster ways were ludicrous.

He had a soft body, a pretty face, two empty eyes. He reminded me of a child.

"But Italo greeted him like a long-lost brother. 'My oldest friend!' he cried. 'My oldest friend! What are you doing here?'

" 'I want to join the bandits,' said the other.

"They began to talk, right there in the midst of us. And gradually, we saw: they'd been childhood pals. And this pretty boy, this nobody—he'd been the leader. Of course things had changed, but it took that fool some time to see it. At first, he still played the bigshot with Italo, teasing him, insulting him a little, saying that our captain wasn't nearly so ugly as he used to be.

"Italo didn't seem to mind. He couldn't have been nicer, or more hospitable. In fact, he told his friend that he could stay as long as he pleased, and showed him to a tent.

"When Italo returned, we gathered round him. 'Send him away,' we said. 'And let's get out of here right now. That man's a fool, he's too soft to ride with us. Besides, he's an informer if we've ever seen one. He can't stay here, we've got to escape, it's dangerous!'

" 'If he's an informer,' Italo said calmly, 'let him go and inform. Meanwhile, my friend's arrival calls for a celebration. Go get the wine we stole from the vineyards up north. Let's drink.'

"Sick with uneasiness, we opened the wine. And that night, we drank until our fear of the informer no longer mattered."

"Suddenly, the foxlike gentleman paused. He looked down at the ground, and wiped his moustache with the back of his hand.

" 'Madame,' he said softly. 'You know the rest of the story yourself. The next morning, we were attacked by an army battalion. Everyone was killed, including Italo Giuliano. In the crossfire, the soldiers accidentally shot their own informer. I alone survived to carry out my leader's wish—to find you, and give you his friendliest regards.'

"For a moment," says my grandmother, "I couldn't speak. Then, I looked at my visitor, and began to scream. 'Of course I know the story,' I screamed. 'The brave outlaw, betrayed by his best friend. I've heard it a thousand times. And that's why I don't believe a single word you say.'

" 'Because Italo Giuliano knew that story too. He'd read it as a boy, in his books. And he would never have walked into such an obvious trap. He knew Italo Salvatore had a hundred reasons for betraying him. He would never have gone along with it, and died such a ridiculous death.'

" 'Besides, I knew you were lying from the beginning. You said that Italo called the stranger his oldest friend. But Italo Giuliano would never have said that. For *I* was his oldest friend!'

"The gentleman stood up. 'I saw it with my own eyes,' he said.

" 'You saw nothing!' I said. 'You're an impostor, seeking charity. You've come here with lies and stolen souvenirs, looking for some kind of pity.'

" 'If Italo didn't die in Sicily,' said the man, 'then where is he?'

" 'He isn't really dead!' I screamed, and slammed the door behind him."

Mrs. Russo takes a deep breath. "Do you really think he's still alive?" she asks. "He'd be old now, like us."

"He promised he'd come back," says my grandmother. "I pray for my husband Anthony among the dead souls. But I pray for Italo Giuliano among the living."

Once again, my grandmother gazes off into the uptown traffic, peering at each passing taxi—as if, at any moment, Italo Giuliano might come riding up, in the back seat of a cab.

"What I want to know," says Mrs. Russo, "is this: Why did he become a bandit? Was it his love for you, his friendship with Italo Salvatore, his homeliness, his reading? Was it all that mistreatment he took as a boy?"

"Those might have been his reasons," replies my grandmother, "but I do not think they were. With a man like Italo there are no simple answers. Mrs. Russo," she sighs, "tell me: Was there ever another man on this earth like Italo Giuliano?"

Mrs. Russo hesitates for several minutes. "Your husband Anthony," she says at last, "was a very good man."

Now the truth of the matter is this: for twenty years Mrs. Russo was in love with my grandmother's husband Anthony. Like her friend, she is a modest woman; so she confined her passion to a few hesitant waves from her window across the courtyard. But once each year, at the Knights of Columbus Ball, she and Anthony danced one waltz. And that is what Mrs. Russo remembers.

And so, every time my grandmother tells the story of Italo Giuliano, Mrs. Russo hears it as the story of her husband Anthony. Whenever she hears it, she understands why that unhappy look came into Anthony's eyes as they waltzed to the orchestra's sad, slow tunes. She understands that it was the look of a man whose wife is married to the memory of a bandit.

Personally, Mrs. Russo couldn't care less about Italo Giuliano. To her, he is no more important than the drunks who stumble across the traffic island.

And that is the true story of bandit lovers—of men like Italo Giuliano, Cartouche, Robin Hood, Lampiao, and Wu Sung.

They never really die. But they can only really live in the hearts of women like me and my grandmother.

U S E F U L

C E R E M O N I E S

At the Passover seder, they are talking about Davy Crockett. All the guests are about the same age and remember the same TV. Perhaps they are thinking of Davy Crockett because of Gail and Maury's country primitive decor. How at home he would feel on their Shaker bench, at their rough-hewn colonial trestle table!

"The Alamo!" says Gail.

"What was he doing there?" Maury asks. "I forget."

"Shopping for a Bowie knife," says Gail's sister Becky.

"Right," Gail says. "Putting it on his American Express."

Becky sets down the spoon with which she's been feeding Gail and Maury's baby, Randy. "Do you know me?" she says, holding up an imaginary card. "Probably you don't recognize me without that stupid raccoon hat."

Everyone laughs, perhaps a bit too heartily; they all know that Becky is having a difficult time. Right now Becky feels okay, tipsy on Manischewitz kirs—"the nostalgia drink," Gail calls it —and tempted to ask: How could they have got through the seder with no one reading from the Haggadah and Davy Crockett in place of Elijah the Prophet? But why criticize? At least Gail and Maury attend their local Reform synagogue. And why be ungrateful when Gail and Maury are letting Becky spend two weeks with them in Tuckahoe, hiding out from her regular life—her loft, her husband Jack, the gallery she and Jack own together?

The last dinner Jack and Becky went to was in a sculptor's Chelsea loft; a Japanese chef made sushi. Becky said, "Don't you think sushi's like some kind of drug? I mean, you get this great protein rush, but six hours later you better eat someting quick or you get suicidal." There was a silence. Then a woman named Darlene sighed and said, "I think sushi's like sex." Later, Darlene got up to go home, and Jack—without a word to Becky—put on his coat and went with her. Darlene's half Malaysian, a critic for a London punk-art journal. It's the least of her problems, but still Becky's horrified that she has been left for a woman with a Mousketeer name.

The brisket Becky's mashing with the back of her fork to feed Randy couldn't be less like sushi; for this alone, Becky feels a rush of warmth toward Gail, who has been saying all week that what got Becky into trouble was asking too many questions. It wasn't the number of questions, thinks Becky, but asking the same one too often.

"Next year," was how Jack always answered. Next year Becky will be forty, and, until the sushi party, had been making a point of it. Jack said he was sorry, he understood, he needed to think more about what having a child would mean. This is what it means, Becky thinks now: meat, plate, fork to mouth. No need to think any further. If only she'd known enough to say that.

"Kentucky," Gail's saying. "No, wait, Tennessee. Kentucky's Daniel Boone."

"Killed him a bear when he was only three," Maury says.

"Three?" Gail says.

"Hear that?" Becky tells baby Randy. "You've got a year and a half."

Gail has talked Becky into collecting books for the temple sisterhood book drive; eventually the books will go to an orphanage in Haifa. Every afternoon, Gail gives Becky a list of names and directions, buckles Randy into his car seat, and sends them out to cruise the suburban streets shaped like horseshoes and keyholes, named for developers' daughters and wives. "Right on Beverly," Becky says to Randy. "Left on Caroline, left on Lorraine."

Mostly it's older women who have signed up to donate books. They all assume that Randy is Becky's baby, and Becky doesn't correct them. The women seem glad to see Becky and Randy instead of the man in the truck they were probably expecting. They invite Becky in for coffee and cake, and Randy, who has a winning personality and can be trusted with an inch in a plastic cup, gets lots of attention and juice.

Becky knows these women. Wednesday afternoons they troop through the gallery by the bus load. At first Becky thought they were only into it for the dressing-up and slumming, but after a while she observed how *interested* they were. Now, seeing their Gropper and Soyer prints, she wonders: Interested in *what*? Becky's most successful artist is a twenty-two-year-old German who makes giant pachinko machines. Sometimes, especially when the women boast about their children's careers, Becky longs to mention the gallery. But personal conversation might lead to her having to admit that Randy isn't her baby, and it doesn't seem worth it. This fantasy they are enacting—that she and the women are joined in some sisterhood of mothers and babies and grown children still present in the high-school earth science texts their mothers are giving Becky—is sweeter than whatever satisfaction she might get from chattering about the art world.

Jack has promised to spend these two weeks moving his things out of their loft. Gail promises he'll come back. Becky has promised Gail that, if he does, she'll just get pregnant and not ask so many questions. For practice, Becky decides not to ask what the orphans in Haifa will do with boxfuls of *Reader's Digest*–condensed Herman Wouks. Not asking lets Becky feel so sincerely appreciative that sometimes tears come to her eyes as she thanks the women for their generosity.

Becky's truly grateful, though not just for the books. She feels some useful ceremony is taking place here, blessing her days with rhythm and purpose—an astonishing feeling for someone whose husband is, perhaps at this very moment, dividing his books and records from hers. Gail knew this would do Becky good; she says Becky needs to get out of herself and plug into a community. Gail was always an expert at conning her—in this case, into picking up books and babysitting Randy at the same time. Still, Becky wonders if Gail might not be right. Perhaps it's the weather, the daffodils and forsythia, the fresh air, but often, driving Randy around to the women's houses, Becky is reminded of the summer she and Jack spent in California, driving their Rent-A-Wreck convertible. She has that same breezy notion that if she just *times* things well, everything will be all right. And maybe that's why it always seems a good omen when, at the end of the afternoon, she pulls into Gail's driveway with Randy so newly and deeply asleep that he can be carried into the house for a long nap in his crib.

Since Becky's been at Gail's, she's taken to mixing herself exotic cocktails she ordinarily wouldn't touch: grasshoppers, brandy Alexanders, and—silently toasting Darlene—Singapore slings. She can't drink very many, but is amazed by how easily they go down, and, if she adds enough alcohol, how optimistic they make her feel. Becky takes a pitcher and glass to Gail's garage and there, among the mulchers and power tools Maury never uses, looks through the books she's collected.

Becky keeps expecting treasure—illustrated children's classics, illuminated prayer books, Victorian medical guides. But now, as always, aside from the high-school texts, it's mostly fifties best sellers, biographies of World War II generals, reports on megacorporations and the CIA. So Becky is astonished when, halfway through her second mango daiquiri, she finds an old edition of *The Legend of Sleepy Hollow*. The book is covered in navy blue silk embossed with gold letters; it weighs a ton and is full of engravings. Turning back to see how they illustrate the Headless Horseman's ride, Becky discovers an envelope. Inside is a note. Even before she reads it, Becky feels that the note was meant for her, that whoever wrote it knew what kind of book would attract her. The note says: "Flexner is killing me. My husband, Lou Flexner, is crazy and trying to kill me. Please help."

The name sounds familiar, but Becky has been to eight houses that afternoon. She goes to the car, where the list of names is still on the front seat. Flexner, Irene, is third from last. Irene Flexner, Becky finally remembers, was the doyenne of a Larchmont Tudor castle, its gray stucco façade so chilly and forbidding it made the interior—the thick white carpeting, the white sectional couches massive and serpentine as the Great Wall—seem doubly lush and inviting. Mrs. Flexner, in a pale linen suit, her platinum hair pulled back in a neat, curled-under ponytail, was perhaps sixty but looked forty-five, like a grandmother in one of those ads with three generations of women all looking terrific.

Mrs. Flexner had gazed at her cooly till Becky mentioned the books. "Of course!" she said "Cutie pie!" she said, leaning close to Randy. "How old is he? She?"

"He," Becky said. "Eighteen months."

"That's the best age," Mrs. Flexner said, "They just *love* you." Then she said, "Come on," and took off across the living room at a speed Becky found particularly impressive because the carpet was so thick and Mrs. Flexner was wearing

such thin high heels. If you could balance on pencils over
three inches of wool, you could do anything! Like so many of
the women Becky has met this week, Mrs. Flexner projected
competence—the energy and nerve to drive the Hutchinson
River Parkway from a book-discussion group to a grocery clear
across Westchester for some treat for a visiting grandchild. If
anyone Becky knew moved that fast, she'd assume they were
on drugs.

Mrs. Flexner paused in the kitchen where a large, middle-
aged black woman was unloading the dishwasher. "This is my
friend Mrs. Nelson," she said. Becky was embarrassed by this
loose use of the word "friend," but Mrs. Nelson nodded
pleasantly and looked past her at Randy, whom she focused
on, cooing musical, Jamaican variations on "Nice little boy."
Randy smiled back at her, quizzical and sweet.

"Mama's big little man," Mrs. Nelson said, and Becky
thought: Mama? If she could fool Mrs. Nelson, she could fool
anyone. She knew this was racist and probably untrue, but still
a rush of good humor stayed with her till Mrs. Flexner, leading
her out of the kitchen past the gleaming Queen Anne dining
room, whispered, "She's been with us forever. She's terrific."
Mrs. Flexner sighed, a sigh rich with knowledge of the in-
justice that makes some women unload others' dishwashers,
and with faith in the human nobility that transcends all that.
Becky was relieved when, pleading a late lunch date, Mrs.
Flexner showed her the books, then called Mrs. Nelson in to
hold Randy while Becky loaded the car.

Becky can hardly believe that stylish, efficient Irene Flexner
could have written that note. She doesn't know what to do
about it, or if she should do anything at all. Rereading it, she

decides that the whole thing depends on how you take the word "kill." "This is killing me," Becky's mother used to say about everything, though what *did* kill her and Becky's father— a drunken teen's '68 Dart—she never even saw coming. Becky opens a book on Jewish law, and skimming a chapter on medieval doctrinal disputes, finds a reference to a Talmudic ruling that it is criminal to know about, and not expose, a crime. Becky takes this as a sign, and though she knows no crime's been committed, has only to imagine a short newspaper item about a Larchmont housewife found dead in the woods near her home.

Becky tiptoes into the house, making the wide board floors squeak. Otherwise it is so quiet she can hear Randy snoring and Gail's potter's wheel whirring in the basement. Standing at the kitchen phone, Becky finds Flexner on Gail's list and dials. When Mrs. Flexner picks up, Becky explains that she was the one who came for the books. Does Mrs. Flexner have any more? There is a silence; Becky is certain that Mrs. Flexner knows she's found the note. "Maybe," Mrs. Flexner says. Then, "Yes. Can you come back tomorrow evening at eight?"

Eight seems like an odd time to pick up books until Becky realizes: dinnertime. Mr. Flexner will almost certainly be home. Is Mrs. Flexner asking Becky to serve as witness and protection?

"All right, eight," Becky says, feeling as if they are speaking in code, two spies out of *Mission Impossible*.

The next day, when Randy asks Becky for his juice bottle, she spends five minutes staring into his diaper bag. She gets lost twice and comes down from an old woman's barricaded Yonkers flat to find she's left Gail's car keys in the ignition. At six, Gail, Becky, and Randy eat an early dinner. Maury is working late. Becky is dizzy from the three White Russians she's drunk, but doesn't want Gail to notice as she asks to use Gail's car. Still Gail could hardly refuse when Becky tells her it's about getting more books.

"Hey," says Gail. "Aren't you working this a little hard?" Becky looks at her but can't quite focus, and Gail, misreading her blurry look, says, "Don't tell me. You met someone. You want the car for a tryst behind the pizza joint at the Mile Square Mall."

Has Becky met anyone? She goes through the faces she saw that day, then the faces of men she thought were attractive when she was with Jack. But Jack's the one she wants to see, wants to tell about the Flexners. As a teenager, she used to imagine boys she liked, dropping in miraculously on cousins' weddings and boring waits at the dentist. Suppose she drove to the mall and there was Jack, signaling her with his lights? He'd only tell her not to go see Mrs. Flexner. What if the husband turns out to be a real psycho?

It's funny, how thinking of Jack has made Becky start feeling afraid. Probably Becky should tell Gail where she's going, just in case, but some part of her refuses to include Gail, to let her have security *and* vicarious adventure. Becky's problems aren't Gail's fault, yet for a moment she resents and envies Gail the safe, dull life she's chosen; Gail doesn't even have to wonder if Maury might not really be working late, if *he* might be the one trysting behind Mile Square Pizza. Becky is on the point of suggesting this possibility or something equally venomous and undeserved, something that will wound Gail and stay between them for months. Could this be the moment for her to bring up a fact they have never discussed: that Maury designs software for a company Gail and Becky both picketed during the Vietnam War? They can be cruel to each other in ways someone else might not register. How does Gail think Becky feels when Gail describes holding newborn baby Randy and wishing time would just stop?

Becky looks out the window; it is already dark. She doesn't see well at night and could easily get lost and drive some cul-de-sac till she runs out of gas. Imagine the relief of calling up and canceling! But this, Becky thinks, is what people mean when they say: I couldn't live with myself if I did. At this hour, there is no way of taking Randy; though Becky will miss his company, she is glad that time has decided for her. If Randy were her child—if she had a child—she probably wouldn't go. Her sense of what risks she could take would change. Perhaps it's better to be unencumbered, to have the freedom to be brave, Becky tells herself, and is instantly demoralized by how small and pitiful her consolations seem.

"Where's your baby?" cries Mrs. Flexner the minute she opens the door. This is the moment for Becky to explain that Randy isn't, strictly speaking, hers. It's like those times when she's forgotten someone's name and hedges, waiting for it to come to her and suddenly there's no turning back; if she doesn't tell the truth, she never can. "My sister's taking care of him," she says.

Becky looks past Mrs. Flexner into the kitchen; Mrs. Nelson

isn't around. She wonders if Mrs. Flexner confides in Mrs. Nelson; if Mrs. Flexner is so afraid, how she must hate to see Mrs. Nelson leave! Becky's imagination is spinning. She reminds herself: This is Westchester, not some misty manor house in *Gaslight* or *Rebecca*. Still, Becky's throat feels tight as Mrs. Flexner ushers her into the living room.

There's a part of the room Becky overlooked this afternoon—a corner where the pastels give way to polished woodwork, bookshelves, gentlemen's club leather chairs. Becky has noticed how little in these houses seems to belong to the men —men tucked away like secrets in dressers full of clean, razor-creased shirts. At least Mr. Flexner has his corner and fills it, just as he completely fills the wing chair in which he sits, reading.

Becky has met dozens of guys like him: sixtyish, slightly overweight, handsome in a way that has less to do with beauty than with confidence, with getting your way in the world. The light from the reading lamp shines on his thick clean white hair, but he also seems lit from within—an aura which makes Becky think it possible to literally radiate success. There's something a little hard about him, an edge of the street smart and tough, but—Becky recalls newspaper photos of suburban execs indicted for putting out contracts on their wives— Flexner isn't a killer. That note must have been metaphorical. Flexner looks up from the *Barrons* he is reading but doesn't stand up.

"This is the young lady from the book drive I told you about," Mrs. Flexner says. "She has the most *beautiful* baby."

"Girl or boy?" Mr. Flexner says. "Not that it matters these days."

"Boy," Becky says, and Mr. Flexner nods. Becky thinks: Well, at least she has the right kind of baby. Then she realizes, with a small shock: she's almost convinced herself Randy's hers.

"We have three," Mrs. Flexner says. "A boy and two girls, all grown. No grandchildren yet." She makes a little pout, then, including Becky, says, "I thought we could all have a bite of dinner. Then I have some more books for you. Come. Keep me company in the kitchen."

Mrs. Flexner won't let Becky help but tells her to sit while she checks the thermometer in the roast and begins cutting iceberg lettuce into chunks. "What does your husband do?" she asks. Briefly, Becky's confused: If she's claimed Gail's baby, should she pretend to her husband too, and talk about Maury's job? "We run an art gallery," she says.

"How fascinating," Mrs. Flexner says. "My husband is a developer. Or anyway, he was. Now he can just sit in his office and play with figures. Well, if that's what makes him happy . . ." Mrs. Flexner smiles; she could be talking about a toddler playing with pots and pans, or maybe Becky just thinks that because that is what Randy may be doing right now. If Becky had stayed at Gail's she could be getting ready to bathe Randy. If only Randy were here! Randy is the one—not Gail, and not Jack—who could get her through this meal. Becky feels a stab of longing, a nearly physical pain. How remarkable that she should miss Randy's body more than Jack's! "Well," Mrs. Flexner says. "Better figures on paper than on girls."

Is Becky supposed to laugh? Is this the moment to mention the note? But now Mrs. Flexner is carving the roast; the whine of her electric knife prohibits conversation. "That meat is done *perfectly*," Becky shouts above the noise. Again, Mrs. Flexner smiles, and as she picks up the platter and lets Becky bring in the salad, the atmosphere is warm and faintly conspiratorial, as if they are children bringing mud pies to Mom and Dad, or concubines bearing delicacies for the shah.

"Food's on!" Mrs. Flexner calls. Her husband lumbers toward the table and takes his seat at its head. Irene serves out the food and suddenly Becky grows dizzy with the sense that she is sitting down with her parents. It has been ten years since their deaths, long enough for Becky to be taken by surprise when she is—as she is now—overcome with missing them.

After a while Irene says, "Lou, Gail's husband has an art gallery in Manhattan." Becky thinks: *Gail's* husband?, then realizes how mixed-up things really are. Gail was the one who first contacted Mrs. Flexner. And Becky has never introduced herself by name.

"Where?" Lou Flexner says. "Art gallery where?"

"SoHo," says Becky. "West Broadway."

Lou Flexner leans back in his chair. "It's all corporate," he says. "More and more. Pretty soon your only customer's going to be the corporation."

"*Corporazione*," Becky says. "Corporate Milan."

Lou Flexner raises one eyebrow; he seems impressed that she can pronounce a five-syllable Italian word. She doesn't even know if it's a real Italian word, but that doesn't seem to matter. He looks at Becky and she looks back, aware that in some funny way they are flirting. Becky concentrates on her plate, and so has her mouth full of roast beef when Lou Flexner says, "So that's where the art money is?" Becky smiles and points to her mouth, turning to Irene as she does so, offering this awkwardness with the food as proof that she is no threat.

"Right," Becky says. "Italians and forty-year-olds who've just inherited the family Honda lot."

"That's my son, any day now," Mr. Flexner says. "Except, with him it'll be the construction business."

"Not any day now," says Mrs. Flexner, and knocks on the wooden table.

"Art's not a bad investment," Becky says.

"Bullshit," says Lou Flexner. "It's a bullshit investment. I'd only buy the stuff if I liked it. You think I'd like it?"

"Sure," says Becky, though it's hard to say what Lou Flexner would make of Rainer's pachinko machines. Liking wouldn't even come into it. "Sure," she repeats, this time with more conviction.

"Maybe I should come down and take a look at it," Lou Flexner says. "Have you got a card?"

"Her and her husband's card," says Mrs. Flexner, stopping Becky, who's reaching into her purse. She does have a card, with her name and Jack's. How would she explain that? "No," she says. "Sorry."

There's a silence. Then Mrs. Flexner says, "You know whose work I especially like?"

"Whose?" asks Becky, checking the walls for a clue.

"Bonnard's," Mrs. Flexner says.

"His paintings are so lovely," Becky says. She knows it's not the most original thing that's ever been said about Bonnard, whose paintings Becky really does like. But what seems important right now is to show some solidarity with Mrs. Flexner.

Mr. Flexner says, "Irene, where did you get the roast?"

"White Plains, I think," she says. "Why?"

"Stringy," her husband says.

"Gail's eating it," Mrs. Flexner says.

Becky looks down at her plate; it's half empty. Gail *could* have eaten it for all the pleasure or nourishment Becky's gotten. Mrs. Flexner says, "I'll tell you something about Bonnard. Something you probably don't know. When his wife died, after forty-six years of marriage, the man just went to pieces! He never painted another nude, never painted much of anything. Four years later he died of a broken heart."

"Irene," says Mr. Flexner. "Stop it."

"That's the difference between Bonnard and the men of today," Mrs. Flexner says. "An artist like that, he knew love, he knew beauty. All today's men know is running around with their thirty year-old secretaries."

It's clear that Mrs. Flexner isn't speaking abstractly. Oh, Becky thinks. Poor Irene. Though running around with a thirty-year-old secretary is better than what Becky might have imagined from Mrs. Flexner's note, it's bad enough. Mrs. Flexner turns to Becky, asking, "Don't you think thirty's a little young for a man my husband's age?"

It occurs to Becky that Mrs. Flexner probably thinks she is thirty, and wants her, by agreeing, to suggest that Flexner is too old for her. Becky is reluctant to hurt Flexner; at the same time she can't help thinking that thirty *does* seem young— especially compared to her age, thirty-nine.

"This isn't the time to talk about this," Flexner says.

"When *is* the time?" asks Irene. "For three days it hasn't been time to talk about you spending the second seder night with her. What did her family think? That you weren't sixty-three and married?" Irene puts her hands over her face and starts to cry. Becky and Flexner look at each other. Suddenly everything is reversed: now they are the parents and Irene the difficult child with whom they must somehow cope. Becky so wants to comfort Irene she has to fight the desire to say: Hey, it happens to everyone. My husband left me for a woman named Darlene.

Irene goes into the kitchen, sobbing louder and more harshly the further away she gets. Even her tears are like a child's—meant for the grown-ups to hear. There are a million questions Becky wants to ask and doesn't, nor does she do what she should do—leave. Instead she sits at the table and stares at Lou. She thinks: Time has stopped, but not at a moment either of them would have chosen. Lou looks slightly past Becky, his face so expressionless she could have caught him deep in thought or glancing in the mirror. Free to examine his face, Becky understands what a thirty-year-old might see there. He can take care of things. He can decide. He and Irene have two daughters and a son.

Strangely, Becky is thinking about the books. Did Irene really have any for her? Is it too late to ask Lou? How nice it would be to have something to take back to Gail's—to sit on the garage floor and let the musty smell of old books intoxicate her, put her into a kind of stupor from which it would be difficult to get up. It's how she used to feel, on hot summer days, sitting on the floor of her mother's attic, looking through boxes of family photos, shuffling those cracked, brown prints of forgotten relatives, courting couples, newlyweds, new babies. Probably those cartons are in Gail's garage. Becky hates it that Gail has inherited them by default. But her loft never seemed safe, permanent enough to house something so irreplaceable. How could she and Jack have had a child if they couldn't even do that?

From the other room, Irene's cries grow more strident and less human. They sound like those distant, oddly aquatic roars that echo from time to time through the zoo, or, Becky realizes with surprise, like *I Love Lucy*'s panicky cry of anxiety and fright. She remembers the last time she heard Lucille Ball make that uncontrolled, rhythmic, animal sound. She even remembers the episode, the one in which Lucy gets a job packing chocolates in a candy factory and the assembly line begins spitting chocolates at her, faster and faster and faster. Becky knows just where she saw it—she can picture herself and Gail lying on their stomachs, their faces cupped in their hands, inches away from the TV screen at the foot of their parents' bed.

The memory is so vivid it summons up much that has happened since, as well as much that should have happened and didn't. And suddenly it's as if all those past and unrealized events are swirling around her, and Becky feels as if she and Lou Flexner are the couple in an insurance commercial she's seen: that cartoon man and woman standing rigid while houses, cars, children, appliances, pets—while all the things there are to lose go on falling behind them like rain.